new boots

louis j. fagan

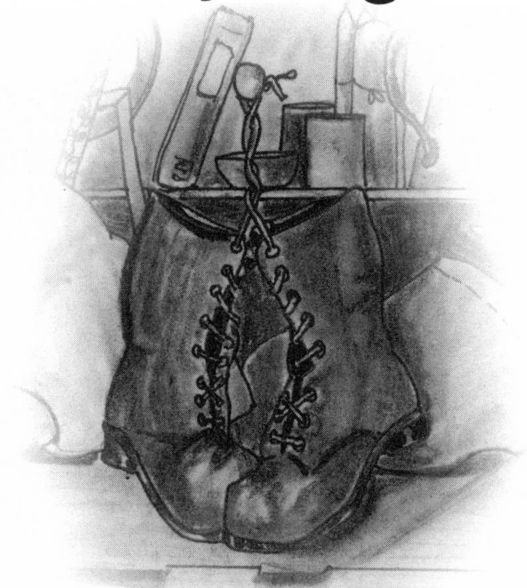

new boots

A-Peak Publishing
Johnstown, NY

A-Peak Publishing
Johnstown, NY

This book is a work of fiction. Names, characters, places, and incidents either are products of the author's imagination or are used fictitiously. Any resemblance to actual events or locales or persons, living or dead, is entirely coincidental.

Printed in the United States of America
First printing: November 1998

Artwork (cover and title page) by Antonio Santana
Design/layout by Chad C. Fleck

Publisher's Cataloging-in-Publication
(Provided by Quality Books, Inc.)

Fagan, Louis John, 1971-
New boots / by Louis J. Fagan. -- 1st ed.
p. cm.
Preassigned LCCN: 98-88221
ISBN: 0-9667407-7-7

1. Adirondack Mountains (N.Y.)--Fiction. I. Title.

PS3556.A3263N49 1999 813'.54
QBI98-1401

To
the ones who believe

new boots

Chapter One

Connie lifted the corner of the thin clear sheet and peeled it from the page. The adhesive squawked and clung, somewhat reverently, to the three photographs that had been neatly placed there in a vertical zigzag fashion.

The yellowness of the years had crept in or down or up the page, but the photographs, they had remained intact. Black and white but as lifelike as the day they had been taken, as vivid, colorful, and expressive as the scenes of her memory.

The page was fully exposed now, and she ran her curving, knobbed-knuckled finger down it, past the top photo of herself on the coast of Ireland. She stopped at the middle one, the one positioned closest to the center and the binding of the book. She felt the top edge of the photo—still a separate entity, she confirmed. Raised, but stuck there. She moved her finger to the corner of it and began to try to pull it from the page, her fingernail working futilely.

Nothing had sent her here today really. She had only one photograph of this man, or, rather, one photograph with him in—

"Mother? Mother, are you up here?" The voice and the sound of footsteps on the stairs came simultaneously.

"Yes, in here, Samantha."

Her daughter was now gray herself with cataracts and children and grandchildren of her own. She moved slowly these days, even more slowly than her own mother did at times, Connie thought to herself. Samantha's marriage of forty-five years to Jerry had been what Connie called "consuming." Jerry drank, Samantha played caretaker. And even after Jerry's death five years earlier, her daughter's existence still seemed to swirl in the wind like a child's pinwheel, sharing its redundant cyclical motion, but lacking, however, the brilliance of one's typically bright silvery colors.

There was something obtrusively different about the sound of Samantha coming up her mother's stairs. And as she rounded the corner and appeared in the open doorway of the bedroom, Connie saw.

"A cane? For Christ's sake, Samantha."

"Mother, the Lord's name," Samantha reminded her mother, as a Sunday schoolteacher would to a cursing child. "How are you today?"

"Doing fine. Looking at this." She glanced down at the open album on her lap. "I worry about the rate at which you're becoming an old lady." Her words were casual and good-natured...because time had taught her how to find and reveal core truths and verbalize them somewhere between the iron cog and milk chocolate.

Samantha smiled and seated herself on Connie's canopy bed, directly across from the reupholstered sofa-chair that Connie was seated in.

The past one-hundred years had shrunk her mother's size, and, in fact, if Connie sat back rather than bent forward over her matter at hand, her head would barely touch the bottom of the intricate white doily that was draped over the back of her chair. But as the flesh speckled and wrinkled and whitened and tightened around her bones, size was all that a century had diminished.

Sunlight poured forth between the two from the open bedroom window, and had Connie looked out, she would have seen one of her great-grandsons with a ladder, making his way across her front lawn. Samantha propped her metal, rubber-stopped cane against Connie's nightstand. "Doctor's orders, Mother. I need this cane. In fact, that's partly why I stopped by," Samantha stretched her smile more, "to show off my fine new walking apparatus."

"Oh, Mother Mary and Jesus. You didn't need it before you went to see him, did yuh?"

"I only hope I can be as half as spry as you are, Mother, when I reach your age." It was true, Samantha admired her mother's strength and spirit. She had tried through her years but felt she had fallen short in that department of her own life. "Maybe strength skips generations," she said matter-of-factly and looked out through the luminous arch of paned glass.

"No, it just shows up in different forms, Samantha."

Connie had done everything right in raising her, both she and Samantha knew this, but still they knew that Samantha had never found her own core truth. Only Connie believed it existed. And now that Jerry had died, Samantha, instead of beginning her overdue search, transferred all her fears and frets upon the old woman who now sat across from her. You will find it when I'm gone, Connie thought and turned her head, too, towards the window then.

The two sat quietly together for a short moment.

"Matthew is here to replace those shingles," Samantha said, turning her face back towards her mother.

Connie cupped her hands together across the photo album as a genuine delight gurgled from within her and surfaced to the pathways of her face, "WONDERFUL, Samantha."

The shingles from beneath her bedroom window had begun to deteriorate from the side of the two-story, estate-turned-farmstead house, and the tuck and nook that they left, in combination with windowpane, had made the ideal home for a hornets' nest. Connie had managed to knock it down earlier that summer but not until after one of its occupants had vamoosed its way into her room through a tattered corner of the screen. She hated killing the little son of a bitch, but he flew wildly around, with his stinger pointed forth she was sure, after her ill-fated attempt to cup it under a glass and rid of it in this humanistic fashion. Yes, Matthew's work would be a necessary precaution against a future episode like this previous one.

Moreover, Matthew was Connie's favorite great-grandchild. His presence at her house had persisted over the years, but girls and school and jobs and his love for travel and writing—especially writing with his countless submissions to and rejections from publishing houses—had their demands on him, and Connie understood this. His dark hair and handsome, stern jaw and full-lipped countenance were a male version of her own youthful reflection.

The two old women heard the clank...clank...clank of the aluminum ladder as it was being extended to its appropriate height. Seconds later, the top of the ladder thudded and leaned against the windowpane, and Matthew was making his way up.

Samantha stood up and stepped to the window and opened the summer screen. Leaning out, she yelled down, "Matthew, you be careful."

Matthew just looked up at his grandmother with her newly set hair and bifocals, and grinned, "I'm not the old lady leaning halfway out a two-story window, Grandma Samantha."

"All the same, Matty Alstrade," she said, working her way carefully back into the house, ducking her head slightly to miss the bottom of the open window. "I'll be off, Mother. Now that Matty is here." Samantha knew of the strong bond between the two, and respected and appreciated it for what it was worth. If only she knew that, regardless of her staying or leaving, she too was a part of the bond—after all, she had mothered the woman who gave birth to the young man soon to poke his head into Connie's room and send forth surges of something that she couldn't quite name. But as Sister Fate so often asks her pupils to wait, Samantha would read of the day's turnings some time later and realize that absence, as we know it, has little to do with presence.

She kissed her mother's face, as did Connie's lips find hers.

She turned and headed for the bedroom door, and Connie glanced at the cane still propped against her nightstand and then back at her daughter, "Dear—"

With her back towards the bed and nightstand and cane, Samantha turned towards Connie. "Yes, Mother?"

"...Drive carefully."

"An old lady like me can drive no other way, Mother." Her words were casual and good-natured, and she left.

Chapter Two

"Hi, Gram."

"Hello, Matthew." Connie shifted in her seat, turning away from her exited daughter to the young man leaning in her window. "Don't you have better things to do on this sunny afternoon than hoist yourself up here to hammer and nail your favorite great-grandmother's falling down house."

"You're my only great-grandmother, Connie, and, no, I don't." Matthew rested his sleeveless elbows on the top of the sides of the ladder. His arms were tanned and he brought them together and rested his head on his big hands. He peered in at the woman garbed in a crocheted vest and pearls. Connie left her silver hair long and pulled it back into a small bun at the base of her head, and Matthew had never seen her wear it any differently.

He unconsciously directed his gaze from his great-grandmother to the back of her chair and her doily, and then to the framed photo on the wall of a family reunion from the seventies, and on to the high ceiling and the slow-paced, rotating ceiling fan, and down to the oak vanity on the opposite side of the room. Everything was just as it had always been in this room, dustless, free of cobwebs and clutter.

He felt like playing with Connie today like when he was seven and would come up and hide under the same pink canopy bed. There he'd remain until the then seventy-two-year-old woman was in such a stir that she'd be forced to yell that she was going to call the volunteer firemen to come and find him if he didn't come out that very instant. His head circled back to his great-grandmother. "Don't you ever mess up your room?...Like throw a keg party or something once in a while...or chase bees?"

The July sun cast a long shadow of Matthew across the hardwood floor, and Connie relished in his presence and thought of the glowing ball behind him. "That little bastard was chasing me, Matthew, so I had to put a finish to him." She clapped the palms of her hands together, and then slapped down on the photo album as it began to slip off her lap. "What about you? How come you're not at LaFette's Beach, chasing girls?"

"C'mon, Gram, why would I want one when I can have them all?" Matthew ran his thumb and forefinger down the two-day stubble on his chin, smiled hard at her, and disengaged his eye contact with his oldest friend. He studied the lines of the floorboards for a second.

She hadn't asked him about MaryAnn in some time because he hadn't mentioned the girl. He had confided in Connie as the two polished off a bottle of Baileys one Christmas Eve a year or two ago. Connie knew somehow that the girl was both there and not there in his life.

"What about that one, the one you told me about?" She pointed her finger in the air as if trying to remember or touch an appellation that floated in front of her in a cloud of women's names that began with M. "Mindy?... Marylyn?...Maura?..."

Matthew knew the fictitious lack of memory was for his benefit, to avoid speaking of her if he wished.

...somewhere between the iron cog and milk chocolate...

"MaryAnn, Gram." He looked back at her.

"Heavens, yes. MaryAnn. You seemed to be pretty crazy about that one the last time you mentioned her, or was that the sauce talkin'?" She winked then. "You don't hear from her anymore?"

The sun was warm on his back and a corner of Matthew's mouth raised involuntarily. "That's a long one, Connie. Maybe over another bottle—or even two—of Baileys."

"Short version?" Connie lifted a brow.

"The last time I saw her, we hadn't seen each other in months and we ended up at this wedding. I have a mutual friend with her man. Complete coincidence—"

"No, fate, Matthew, fate. And...?"

"And when we had a second alone together, I confessed my undying love...Of course, I was three sheets to the wind—"

"Of course."

"There was nothing like the times that we had spent together. Amazing, yuh know? And I just wanted to hear her admit it, and she couldn't say anything. And when she finally did all it was was—I think I should get your number. I said no, I think that's a bad idea......her boyfriend walked over and they left."

"She had something to say, Matt, she just couldn't find the words just then. We're like that sometimes."

Two sparrows, chirping wildly, darted in and out of one another's path and flew behind Matthew. A chorus of songbirds had landed in the maple a few yards from the window, as well, and Matthew turned his head towards them and then back to Connie. He swayed his head to the side, "Maybe."

They would talk of it later.

He looked in the room, at the hands of his great-grandmother's alarm clock that was sitting on her nightstand. "Better get this started. You're paying me by the hour, right?" he said and headed back down the ladder for a hammer to remove the several nails that once bore the siding and, now, either held a dangling shingle or protruded lonely from beneath the pane.

Connie didn't hear the sound of Matthew's feet making their way up the aluminum ladder, nor did she see the top of it move slightly as it adjusted itself to the weight of his body. In fact, she was still surveying the busy photo when Matthew's upper-body appeared in her window.

As Matthew began pulling out the nails, he looked up at Connie who was stooped closely over her album. "What yuh got there, Gram?" Interested in both his repairs and what was enchanting his great-grandmother, he looked down at his work and pulled a nail out of the claw of his hammer.

Connie returned to 1994. "Matthew, could I trouble you for one more thing?"

The central photograph and Connie's main point of interest still lie stiffly adhered to the album's page, and her earlier efforts to remove it had resulted in a slight cut under her delicate fingernail and a crumpled corner. Goddamn whoever thrust a good portion of a lifetime of photos—all out of order for that matter—into this thing, just as well in the dated envelopes I had them in, Connie cursed softly, and with no real conviction, to herself.

Matthew had reached inside and set a few crooked nails and the hammer next to the window and nightstand, and was working his way into Connie's room. His long legs, covered with faded Levi's, and his size ten feet, snugged in his worn tan workboots, stuck half out the window, as he crawled in head and hands first. "What we got here?" he said, lifting himself off the floor and squatting next to the arm of Connie's chair. "That's you?" He pointed to the top photo of the young girl, who, with parasol in hand, was standing on what appeared to be a sunny but windy coast.

"Yes, that's me." Connie focused her gaze on the top photo. "I was fifteen then. Father had taken the family to Ireland for the summer..."

Matthew whistled.

"Yes, yes. Well, father kept a close watch on me back then, so my...handsomeness did me little good." She patted the hand Matthew had placed on the head of the chair's arm. He continued to look at the photo, but Connie had been distracted from her purpose long enough. "But, Matthew," she diverted his attention with her finger as she pointed to the photo, "it is this photo that I ask you to remove for me so that I may have a closer look."

Matthew glanced at the photo—one of some sort of picnic, around the turn of the century, he guessed—and then looked up at Connie. As he had witnessed earlier, she had submersed herself in the world that the 3-½ X 2-½ black and white contained.

He said nothing as he leaned forward and worked his fingernail under a corner of the photo. The scratchy zzzipping sound of the photo being removed from the sticky page quickly followed, and Matthew held the scene up for his great-grandmother to study more closely.

While she was stooped over, her eyes hadn't been able to focus on or clearly define whom she was so intent on finding in this sea of faces. But as she took the photo from Matthew's hand and drew it closer, her vision danced in the detail. The top hats and long dresses and patches of grass and checkered blankets and picnic baskets. Matthew watched Connie's eyes bounce from point to point, up and down, and back and forth across the photo. He gave her a few more moments. "Gram?"

She had heard her great-grandson just as she moved her search to the far top right corner of the photo where a figure of a man was carrying a crate just beyond the crowd's furthest edge. His image was practically distorted by his distance from the camera's lens and that day's rising heat, still here it existed on the photographer's paper.

"GRAM."

Connie, still holding the photo, turned her head towards Matthew. "Are you sure?" she asked.

He nodded.

"You have time?"

He nodded affirmatively again.

She looked back at the photo and adjusted her eyes once again. "I was seventeen when this was taken. Two days earlier......"

Chapter Three

Music was bursting from a band underneath a small wooden gazebo just to the left of the station. Mr. Pottash certainly had went all out, and she secretly thanked him to herself, for the notes of the brass and strings that seduced her ears. This was not symphony as she had experienced in the family's confining box at Rhyme's Theater nor was it anything like the stuffy pieces that were only allowed on her father's victrola. No, this, on the contrary, was quite...... momentous music—flavored with vinegar and glasses of porter.

The year was 1911. July second. And just the thought of their first visit to this mountainous haven raptured bodily pleasure in the young girl. Months earlier, millionaire and friend of the family, Mr. Thomas Pottash had invited the McRamsees to the grand opening of The Water's Edge Inn, a resort he had playfully nestled in the heart of the Adirondacks with what he called "a few extra thou that just must be spent."

And, now, here, three months later, she was standing on the steps of a steam train and living only what she could not quite have fully imagined while sitting with a needlepoint hoop in the annoyingly posh hilltop estate on Prisonna Street. Breathing this air, air that was still cluttered with the coalish fumes of the train's engine and a few hundred people milling about, but air nonetheless, resounded much differently in her lungs, this she was sure of already. She could not, however, quite place that difference from the air of where she lived or from all the other places she had visited, and so attempted to take another deep breath. With shoulders slighting back, she pulled a mouthful into her lungs and—

"Cornelia. Cornelia, darling, we mustn't stand here the entire day," Mrs. McRamsee said into her daughter's right ear from the step above her. Cornelia felt the sharpness of her mother's voice and the soft of the large peacock plume that swooped across the tight-lipped woman's wide-brimmed hat as it brushed her left cheek.

"Yes, Mother. Of course." She withheld an inner-laugh that had been invoked by both the mountain air and the sensation from the feather's tickle, for she knew that her mother would demand justification for this simple sign of pleasure.

Too often, in their parlor, as her mother and lady guests drank tepid tea and discussed, say, the most God awful linens of Miss Bertha Flachmieir's dress as seen at the opera the previous night, Cornelia would be seated with her legs pressed perpendicular to the floor and holding a piece of the fine Parisian china. She would stare out the picture window beyond the brick and roofs to the distance where sky met the Hudson River, and think of a sea gull far from its ocean home and engaged in flight and bathed in the blue, one that might kindly fly through her sitting room window, smashing the glass upon its entrance, and shit directly into the tea cup of one of these pretentious old biddies with whom she sat. Perhaps, the gob of gray and white shit might land in her own mother's cup, and, at this and the thought of the women's faces, Cornelia's inner-laugh would curve her lips upward and force her to cover an approaching snicker with a ladylike cough. And having drawn her mother's attention, she most surely would be subjected to "Dear Cornelia, what is it you would like to add?" and she could not talk about the sea gull and his bowel movement, but would be forced to raise a completely different curtain of her imagination: "Why Mother, Miss Mary Ellen Hendrason's dress at her party three nights past was just as dreadful" she might say and slip back into the skyline.

Today, Cornelia did not want to be bothered with her mother's judgements or postulations. There was something to these mountains that surrounded this small station that seemingly sat in the middle of wilderness.

Cornelia lifted the pleats of her pale purple dress and stepped off the train onto a rectangular man-made wooden step and then to the planked station platform. She smiled cordially to the man who stood erect and with his arms at his sides. An Arborlines Railroads employee and, perhaps, proud owner of the nifty wooden crate-turned-portable step, Cornelia thought. A thick black moustache sat atop his returning smile. "Your father wishes me to tell you that your belongings are being loaded in an inn car on the opposite side of the station, and he has asked me to point your mother and you in that direction," he said, with one arm and finger extended now. "Simply head through those doors."

Cornelia's mother had descended the steps, as well, and, having heard enough of the gentleman's words, nodded and gave a "Very well, sir" without turning her head.

She slipped her arm into Cornelia's and steered them towards the open doors of the shoebox station. Having been quickly shuffled off, Cornelia turned back to say thank you, but people were traipsing to and fro between her and the man by now and she deemed it necessary to raise her arm, her white-gloved hand, and her voice—"Thank you, sir!" The train whistle blew and the porter did not hear her, and for a moment, she resented her father's handing of money to this man and announcing their arrival to him as if they were the First Family.

"Dreadfully hot here," her mother remarked half to herself, half to Cornelia, as she continued to lead her daughter through the crowd, through the doors, and to the less busy side of the station.

Dreadful would not be the word I would use, thought Cornelia. As they quickly walked through the station—no more than a room with a few benches and a ticket window—and found themselves on the steps of an unshaded porch, Cornelia raised her hand to her eyebrows and squinted towards the sun. The hot, glowing ball of bright pale yellow and orange and white was on the downside of its daily journey to the western edge of the sky, but, nonetheless, still, perhaps, four man-made hours from its setting place. No, it was not dreadful.

The dirt road—stretching in both directions and running somewhat, it seemed, parallel to the railroad tracks at least for a few hundred feet from the station until pines and forests separated the two means of transportation—was lined with a fleet of what the porter had called inn cars.

CHAPTER FOUR

Mr. Pottash had sent more than three dozen shiny new Fords to pick up his guests. Personal servants and employees of The Water's Edge Inn strapped and stacked valises, trunks, and suitcases in and on the cars, as most of the men, garbed in top hats and lengthy suit jackets, stood alongside of the vehicles in groups of four or five. They smoked their cigars, rolled from Cuban finest, and boasted of this or that latest business venture, be it coal or oil or textiles or diamonds. Some suggested their wives had packed too much for the summer's stay, others bitched about the servants' carelessness with the possessions, and most congratulated Pottash on his brilliant investment as he sauntered from group to group. His exclusive guests this summer would break the place in, give it a name, set the trend for summers to follow. Pottash had a head for business. Must have had the railroad lay track and land a station here in the nowhere just for his latest girl, The Water's Edge Inn, some whispered.

A few women lingered in the station or on the porch, while many attempted to repudiate the intense heat of the afternoon by quickly curtseying to other guests and taking to their designated cars.

Mr. McRamsee, standing in a tight circle with a few other men, raised the brass handle of his walking stick when he saw his women exit the train station. Sweat formed above his brow and a few beads wandered down his white temples as he too savored a fat cigar that Robert Stimes had just handed him.

"Your daughter grows lovelier and lovelier each time I see her, Henry. Do say you haven't betrothed her to anyone just yet." Robert stuck his cigar in his mouth and pulled his cheeks in tightly to suck on a mouthful of smoke. He had been in Paris for the spring and South Africa before the holidays, forever building the best mine or adding royally-crafted gold and diamonds and rubies to a collection started by his great-grandfather—a man whose wealth and jewels could do little to save his fleeting sanity, but one whom Robert revered deeply, nonetheless. Mr. Stimes had not seen McRamsee, or the family, since last autumn on the Cape.

"Ahh, Stimes does have an eye for jewels, doesn't he, gentlemen?" Mr. McRamsee nudged the youngest member (and his most favorite) of the old money club and winked, and all the men roared with laughter and said things like "That he does" and "Indeed, she is a fine young lady."

"Robert, there is nothing I'd like more than to see you at my house for the holidays. Perhaps, we can work on that this summer, aye?" Henry added, with another soft elbow to the hopeful suitor's side.

In truth, both men wanted nothing more.

Mrs. McRamsee spotted her husband upon his signaling and started down the stairs with their daughter close beside her. Cornelia had been looking in another direction when she felt her mother's tug. The people and the cars and the field of swaying buttercups directly across from the station had been Cornelia's key points of interest, not her father's locale.

The two women worked their way through the assemblage of guests, and Mr. McRamsee's circle had begun to disperse just before their arrival.

Gentlemen joined their women, or rounded them up, and sifted into their cars. Chauffeurs honked and engines turned over.

"Dear Lord, you ladies would be late for a sold-out appearance of the Messiah Himself," McRamsee attempted at humor, mostly for the benefit of his remaining comrade than for the women. He dropped his half-smoked cigar in the pebbles below their feet, and Mrs. McRamsee ignored his remark, "Why, Mr. Stimes, it is a pleasure to see you safely back here in the States."

She extended her arm, and Stimes bowed graciously and kissed her white-gloved knuckles. "The pleasure is all mine, Mrs. McRamsee."

He directed his speech to the McRamsee daughter whose attention, at the moment, was grappling the steep incline beyond the meadow. "And Miss Cornelia, you put these wild flowers to shame. How are you?"

The touch of his hand on hers induced her to turn her head towards the source. "Good day, Mr. Stimes. How nice to see you again." Cornelia had known Robert Stimes since she was a child of ten or eleven. He was twenty years her senior, and his blatant interest in her did not *completely* appall her…however, his recent wooing on the Cape, and that which, she suspected, would surely surmount here—in truth, she wanted nothing less.

"Won't you join me in a day or two, once you are settled in, for some target shooting, or perhaps, some live game will run or fly our way, if we are so fortunate, and we can take a crack at that?" Stimes directed his question now to the whole McRamsee family.

"Why, of course, Robert. We're anxious to witness another round of your excellent marksmanship as we did last summer" followed from the McRamsee patriarch. Mrs. McRamsee nodded in approval, as well.

A Water's Edge Inn driver stepped behind the group then. "Mr. McRamsee, the car is ready when you are, sir."

"Very well, Roland. Let's be off."

Several of the cars and their occupants had begun to pull away from the edge of the road and were now heading towards the resort.

"I really must return to my car, as well." Mr. Stimes shook McRamsee's hand and nodded to the females. "Until the next time, ladies."

The McRamsees, like Mr. Stimes, like all of Pottash's other prominent guests, piled into the plush seats of their car. The ride would last nearly an hour and a half, and the extravagance of the latest Ford model would do little to ease the jostling incurred upon its wealthy occupants from the rough road…

"Not long now, just got word they'll be up in little over an hour!" a loud, pear-shaped woman in a bright blue servant's dress yelled as she carried a basket of white linens across the green lawn in front of The Water's Edge Inn. Miss Eliza Stewart headed the staff and had seen to the hiring of each of Pottash's employees, or the goodly lot of them anyway, everyone from the musicians to the floor scrubbers, the cooks, the laundresses, and the shitshovellers. All Water's Edge workers had sat down to at least a two minute interview with Miss Eliza.

As twenty-five percent of America's richest zigzagged their way through the woods and mountains of the Adirondacks, the other side of life prepared for their arrival. Tables were being set up behind the three-story dollhouse. White tablecloths bordered with lace were being swooped over them by the mostly young servant squad. Silver trays of fresh salmon pâté and pastries and caviar sat atop the steady hands and shoulders of young men in crisp white shirts and bow ties. Bottles of wine and champagne awaited Pottash's playmates.

Further on, beyond the back lawn and behind the six foot high, lengthy strip of sculpted shrubbery lay the stable area, corral, and small barns. One of the stableboys had relayed Miss Stewart's announcement to his co-workers and each were expected to finish the detail that had been assigned to him and report to Stewart later that evening.

"Finish up, Flint!" Wemple, a weasely-looking fellow blurted as he sped through the cow barn.

"Tell her that, Wemple, not me," the young man said over his shoulder, giving a nod to the Guernsey milking cow that stood before him. He sat on a three-legged milking stool and pulled at the cow's udder, and like all others, had sat with Miss Stewart about the work at hand. "Mr. Flint you certainly are a charming, good-looking young fellow who might be more suitable to wait the tables than shovel horse dung," Stewart, several weeks earlier, surmised aloud as she concluded her slightly extended interview with the native from the foothills of the Adirondacks.

His parents had sold their farm to the government, as the land they were on was to be flooded for a recreational reservoir, and he had headed into the heart of the mountains upon hearing that the richies were in need of people who knew the mountains and were willing to pay quite well for areas of expertise, his being horses, cows, soil, and, as Miss Eliza quickly recognized, people.

Upon Miss Stewart's suggestion, Samuel begged her pardon in declining her offer and persuaded her that he would be much more content and of use to her, and her boss, if he follied behind the shrubbery. She agreed, and he headed for the "equestrian hands' quarters" she had pointed out—with a wink and a mock lofty voice—that was tucked in the wood and behind the horse corral.

The cow lifted her leg slightly, tapping the bucket beneath her. "Eeeeasy, girl...or you want ol' Miss Stewart to come out here and tug on you herself."

The cow turned its head and stopped chewing its cud for a moment as it looked at the hand who sat beside her, talking to her. "Yeah, didn't think so," he said and then blew a puff of breath out and up to unstick the sweaty hair that pressed to his forehead.

Taking two more squirts of milk and pulling the nearly full bucket out from underneath the animal, a scroll of The Water's Edge Inn rules and regulations appeared in Samuel's head. He set the bucket on the barn floor, and rolled down his sleeves and buttoned his cuffs. "You're the easy end of this deal, girl." He grabbed the handle, headed past the shrubs, and delivered his bucket to The Water's Edge Inn kitchen well before any of the guests arrived.

Chapter Five

Pottash's welcoming reception had been nothing she hadn't experienced more than enough times before that day, except for the fact that it was held in a cradle of the summer-sprawled, majestic Adirondacks. Corks flew, and trays after trays were taken away and re-smeared with stacks of delicacies. Cornelia shocked herself with her own surprise at the indifference of the people gathered here. They ignored the birds' voices, the century old pines, and the full oaks with leaves the size of three hands. Even the setting sun as it bathed and then blanketed violets and pinks across the mountain tops, preparing them for a night's sleep, turned few heads.

Still, the peaks glowed softly in the dim light of the low-hung crescent moon. Robert Stimes had grown more and more persistent with each crystal glass of deep red wine he drank, and when his tank was overflowing and the toilet called, Cornelia feigned fatigue and excused herself.

At home the lights from the harbor and boats and street lamps infringed upon Cornelia's plight to view the summer stars, but here, if she wandered just far enough away from The Water's Edge Inn tonight, she could savor their spirited presence.

She could not label the summer constellations, knowing only the Big Dipper and the North Star, but labeling them was not her intention. The stars, she believed, could not be mapped, this merely man's effort to tame them. They could not act as a postmark or street address for whom they shone down upon, their power too great and purposeful for deeds so trivial. Cornelia wished only to behold the specks of light that, in the books she had read, led kings on horseback and granted lovers fiery gifts—how these distant celestial bodies could ignite dormant desires deep within, her girlhood ache to ride as those chosen few had, her wonder and want of that feeling only man and woman could share.

Rather than the tap, tap, tap of her boots on the cobbled stone walks of her city, her soles swished through the cut grass and her heels left tiny round imprints as they momentarily became one with the ground over and over again. The silence swooned her and, through it, a grove of maples to the side of the inn whispered her name. She went.

Encircled by outstretched limbs, she lay on the yet warm grass and looked up at a new sky. She found her own patterns and configurations of light in the darkness above her, and watched them ease their way across the space, having no idea of how they slowly sped.

She retreated to bed after an hour or so, knowing the trouble that would follow if she were not there when she was looked in upon by her parents…

…and so, here, she lay the next morning, awake with the sun rather high in the east and with the stars and night sky still etched on her inner-thought.

Her first full day at The Water's Edge would be routine and she knew this, welcomed it really, because the sooner it was over, the closer she was to disappearing from the tea times and gossip and advancements of rich men. She would be expected and then disregarded, and this suited her.

She bathed and dressed and descended to the breakfast room on the first floor. She entered the double doors and a servant pointed her to a table at which her parents were already seated. Breakfast would be a hobnobbing ritual with stops at the table by other guests, close friends of the McRamsees and those wanting to be close friends. Jokes about how much alcohol was consumed the previous night and invitations would be made. But the position of the table and the small book that Cornelia had tucked in her velvet handbag would ease her ache to venture out of doors, away from her typical world.

The table sat on the far end of the room, closest to the kitchen and directly next to three huge frames of glass that were more like a wall in size than a window. The back lawn looked as if there had been no celebration there last night. Water's Edge Inn servants scurried about with lawn chairs and huge sun umbrellas, and some guests had begun to explore the grounds.

But beyond the lawn lay the mountains, towering and bright with forest green, already cupping the day's warmth.

"Good morning, darling," Mrs. McRamsee rose and kissed her daughter. Mr. McRamsee had arisen too, but his greeting was overshadowed by his fowl breath and sunk-in eyes. Father *had* talked rather loudly last night, Cornelia thought.

"Good morning, Mother. Father." They seated themselves,

Cornelia facing the clear glass and natural scene.

Mr. McRamsee signaled a servant, and a glass of orange juice arrived for Cornelia shortly after. "Thank you," she said and sipped.

"Henry, Mrs. Lawrence asked Cornelia and I to join her for lunch just past noon, and I would imagine some of the other ladies will be stopping by for a visit, as well. Now, had you decided..." Mrs. McRamsee's words continued, followed by those of Mr. McRamsee and the conversation moved forward as such.

But to Cornelia, as she studied the going-ons outside before her—moving her eyes from the colorful umbrellas being propped up to the arbitrary straightening of bow ties and wrinkled dresses by the young, nervous servants—the sea of her parents' words became less clearly defined, as if rocking and sloshing back and forth in...in a bucket.

A bucket......her eyes landed upon a tin bucket and she followed the strong hand that held its handle up, and passed the gray-sleeved arm, to a shoulder and a face. She watched as the young man, quite close to her in distance by now and seemingly headed for the back door of the kitchen, nodded and smiled at fellow workers as he passed one or two of them. His hair was sandy brown, with light streaks of yellow from the summer sun and his smile...he seemed to use his whole face when he curved his lips upward. She followed his movements, connecting his face to his shoulder again, then his suspenders and his pants and then his feet, as he passed just a few yards on the opposite side of the glass into the outer servants' entrance of the kitchen. She noticed he did not dress like the other servants with a bow tie and a starched white shirt, the clothes he wore were his own, it seemed, and his left boot, close to where his little toe would be, had a visible hole in it.

Samuel Flint walked through the open back door of the suffocating kitchen. Steam and heat rose everywhere, and cooks and servants busied themselves preparing eggs and sausage and coffee. They sliced fresh fruit and heaped it on trays and exited through the swinging doors into the breakfast room. And no one seemed to notice his entrance, except for Miss Stewart who had been leaning over a vat of steaming something. "Mr. Flint. Good morning to you. And you've brought me another bucket of cream, I hope?" She walked towards him with her wooden spoon in her hand. She gave a servant girl a quick whack on her ass, as the girl seemed to be leaning over a counter, head in hands and half dozing. The youngster erected herself immediately and darted off with a full tray of biscuits that had been sitting beside her. "Get your ass goin', girl." Stewart's words chased her out the door. "We run a tight ship around here, Mr. Flint."

"I see that Miss Stewart. How do you do this morning?"

She was standing in front of him now. "Very well, thank you. However, the last bucket you brought in earlier this morning—well, Mr. Flint, it had cow—there was some—"

"Cow shit, ma'am?"

"Yes, Samuel, cow shit on the bottom of the bucket and that just won't do, will it." She leaned a little closer, lowering her voice, "And Pottash would give me a crack on *my* ass if the likes of that smell lingered out there in that room, yuh see. Could you imagine some of their puckered-up faces?" Samuel reflexively hunched forward a little as she gave him a smack with her spoon in his gut. She leaned back and laughed. "So, I've furnished you with that there crate, dipper and bottles are in it," she pointed to the corner of the kitchen behind Samuel where a wooden crate sat, "and you can pour your milk in there and run that over here instead of that damned ol' bucket that spends half its time under those Guernseys."

"What pleases you, Miss Stewart, works for me," Samuel said and winked.

"Ohhh, you're tryin' to win my heart, Mr. Flint. You'll work out fine here, just as I thought you would." And with that, Miss Stewart turned away and headed back to her boiling vat.

By then, a servant boy had noticed Samuel's entrance and had taken the bucket and dumped its contents in a pot in the back of the kitchen. He returned and set the bucket next to Samuel's feet, just as Miss Stewart had finished.

"Thank you, Willy," Samuel said, and left the kitchen with the bucket in right hand and crate on left shoulder.

He again crossed a short distance from the wall of glass and Cornelia immediately shifted her wandering gaze back to him. She watched as he strode by.

While Samuel made his way past the breakfast room, he felt, as he had felt heading towards the kitchen, the same sensation—that someone was watching his movements. The sun cast a slow, steady glare already this morning, but Samuel instinctively turned his head into it and to where he considered might be the source of an intent stare.

As his eyes peered through the window for a brief second, he saw the outline of a woman, a woman who he saw quickly glance away and pick up a glass in front of her—

"Cornelia. Cornelia, dear?" As always, Mrs. McRamsee searched for the reason of her daughter's strange behavior and glimpsed outside only to find servants and guests here and there and a livery hand making his way back to the stables. She turned back to Cornelia. "Your father is talking to you, dear."

Cornelia took another sip of juice. "Yes, father, I'm sorry."

"Must be the mountain air." Mr. McRamsee's hangover was subsiding, and he attempted to make light with his daughter, putting his hand on hers. "Connie, later this afternoon, Robert Stimes has asked us to join him on the target range Pottash has set up for him. I've accepted the invitation and do hope you will meet us there at three—promptly at three."

"Henry, you do know how I dislike when you call her Connie, and she will be with me for the most part of the day, so we will both be there—on time."

Connie took another sip of juice and politely pushed a

smile across her face.

"Wonderful, then." Mr. McRamsee stood, kissed his wife and his daughter, and excused himself for a day of cavorting with the other gentlemen.

The afternoon passed just as Mrs. McRamsee had promised her husband. After breakfast, she and Cornelia returned to their suite and freshened for lunch. The process took nearly an hour and a half as the two women's personal servants, Beatrice and Lucinda, re-ruffled their dresses, applied powders and perfumes, and reset their hair for them.

The McRamsee women joined Mrs. Mary Francis Lawrence, wife of the oil tycoon Steven B. Lawrence, and a circle of three or four other important women precisely at twelve-thirty on the front lawn for a four course lunch of Pottash's finest fresh fish and poultry, cheeses and vegetables, cinnamon teas and murky mineral waters. Each piece of food was commented on and approved or disapproved by the women, and from time to time, Cornelia would smile, as if interested, and look to the sky as pure white clouds mockingly floated by. Today the oh-so glorious gun show, she thought, and tomorrow the grand picnic, and the day after, that will be when my presence will not be so missed. Appearances these first few days, it was customary wherever they went.

Mrs. Lawrence leaned close to Mrs. McRamsee, while the other women talked of their husbands' money, "Julia, dearest, Cornelia is such a timid girl. Why, I have barely heard a peep out of her all afternoon."

Mrs. McRamsee was all too used to inquiries into her daughter's behavior. "Oh, Mary Francis, Henry and I do hope she comes around this summer. She spends so much time in the city park or closed up in her room reading or painting." She looked across the table at her daughter who was listening to Katherine Bointon tell of Mr. Bointon's real estate investments in the South. "We're not fretting, Mary.

She is a beautiful girl, and Mr. Stimes has always had a great interest in her. She will be fine."

The sun danced across the sky.

The group of ladies began to dissipate.

Mary Francis excused herself for afternoon prayer at The Water's Edge Inn Chapel—though not without first expressing how delighted she was that Mr. Pottash had recognized the importance of Jesus in some people's lives—and then reported she would join the McRamsee women at the shooting range shortly after.

Quite a crowd of both men and women had gathered on the north end of the grounds when Mrs. McRamsee and Cornelia arrived. Some chairs had been scattered about, and, to Cornelia, Robert Stimes appeared as some sort of conductor in front of a muddled orchestra. With his batons, a rifle and a pistol, in either hand, he tipped his hat with the silver barrel of the smaller gun to the two ladies as he saw them approaching. He stuck the handgun in a leather holster at his side, and walked towards them.

"Won't you ladies move to the front of the masses. I do not know where they have all come from," he said, after working his way to the tail-end of the richly gathering.

He loves his guns, Cornelia thought, because he has no gun of his own, and he knows where all the sightseers came from, he couldn't have been *that* drunk as he ran his mouth last night begging people to come see him shoot.

"Perhaps we should join your father, Cornelia..." Mrs. McRamsee said, looking over and between people to see her husband with brandy and cigar in hand and alongside several other men at the front of the group.

"Mother, I don't think Mrs. Lawrence will find us through all these spectators once Mr. Stimes's exhibition of marksmanship begins, so, perhaps, we should stay here in the rear of the group." Connie smiled at Stimes.

"Yes, it would be rather rude of us to invite Mary

Francis and then abandon her. I hope you are not too terribly disappointed, Mr. Stimes. We will cheer for you from back here."

Stimes took this setback with ease and set the neck of the long rifle atop his shoulder. "Very well then, ladies, please enjoy yourselves. I'll let Mr. McRamsee know you are here." He bowed and stepped away from the two and retreated back towards the front of the crowd.

A few more prospective viewers crossed the lawn to where the now rather large group sat and stood, and as Stimes reappeared at the head of the small aggregation—or congregation, in his thought—and in everyone's view, a sort of shhh and hush happened. Overtrained observers of operettas, the star was in the house, the show about to begin.

Only a crow continued to caw from a nearby tree.

Robert turned fully towards his audience. "Well, good afternoon, ladies and gentlemen. What started out as a short hour on the target range has turned into a Water's Edge Inn circus of sorts." Approving laughter from those before him. "And it appears I am the ringmaster." Another wave whished forward, and Cornelia's stomach turned some as she watched Stimes flutter-kicking along in it.

"Have I missed anything?" Mrs. Lawrence whispered in between the McRamsee ladies' heads. She had swept her way across the lawn in a hurry, fearing more that she would be at a loss at dinner that evening as all the important guests would be recollecting key moments from Mr. Robert Stimes's shooting show than the fact that she may actually miss the live event. In this case, Jesus could be worshipped in brief.

"Mr. Stimes is about to begin," Mrs. McRamsee answered.

The range extended for what appeared, to Cornelia, to be almost a mile. Small handcrafted clay animals sat on short wooden stands, the closest one being one-hundred feet off to the far left side. Cornelia made out the vague shape of a rabbit on his hind legs. Further back and to the right sat another stand and clay animal. And a distance behind that and to the right, another, and then another, and still another. Five in all.

Stimes handed his rifle to a small black boy, perhaps eleven or twelve, who was dressed in a Water's Edge uniform and standing close by. The boy stepped back, as if holding the Holy Grail, and gave room to the gunman. Stimes pulled his pistol out of his holster and aimed. Less than a second later, a thunderous crack and the first and closest clay rabbit shattered into pieces. The next four followed shortly after, as Stimes angled himself further right just a notch each time and fired, never missing his mark.

As the last miniscule figurine cracked and crashed, the crow who quieted for nothing a few moments earlier flew from his tree, at least a half mile off, and crossed the range. Mr. Robert Stimes then finished his round so naturally, so casually, that many thought the gregarious black-feathered beast simply must be a part of the act. Stimes cranked his arm up, aimed for the eye of the crow and, with ease, blew the head from the body in motion.

The creature fell to the ground before the echo of the firearm faded, and the thump of the three-pound bird hitting trimmed grass could not be heard over the clapping crowd.

Stimes turned and gave an engaged bow and quieted his fans with his extended finger. He holstered his pistol and signaled for the young servant to bring the rifle over. The boy obediently stepped forward and handed the gun over, and Stimes leaned into him to whisper something in his ear.

"I'm sorry?" the boy said, his voice carrying longer and louder than he had expected by the look of his countenance.

Stimes impetuously slapped him across the face and then smiled quickly and patted his shoulder. He reached inside his coat pocket, pulled out an apple and handed it to the child, and then pushed him on the rump.

Everyone watched as the white-suited little boy became a porcelain doll who reached up and then placed and balanced a speck of red on his head at the opposite end of the range.

Stimes turned just for one second towards his followers. They gazed at him as if he swung a pendulum in front of their eyes. He turned back towards his target, raising his rifle.

The boom.

The splintering of the fruit.

The applause.

Only one did not raise her hands.

...Stimes was guest of honor and sat at a head table during dinner that evening, the latter much to the satisfaction of the youngest McRamsee.

And as a knightly twilight alighted on The Water's Edge Inn, Cornelia recognized rescue and retired to her bedroom early—or, that is, as early as an accordance with etiquette's approval allowed her.

From her second floor private balcony, she heard Mr. Robert Stimes's words as he entered the first floor study with some other men to drink and smoke. He leaned into his circle of confidants and began a story with "Well, as far as that little impudent nigger's actions today..."

...Cornelia thwarted Robert Stimes and his advances in her dreams that night, waking in heavy, warm sweat and pulling her pasted, wet hair from her face...

Chapter Six

"Hell of a day for a shindig, aye, Mikey?" Samuel sat, buttoning his shirt, on the edge of his bottom bunk. He shared a small one-windowed room, no more than a ten by ten, furnished with two bunk-beds and a water basin, in the livery hands' quarters with another young man about three or four years younger than him.

Michael Truman wasn't a bad person with whom to share a room. He snored and he farted in his sleep from the top bunk, but for the most part he seemed good-natured. His sisters and brothers, eleven in all, and his mother lived in New York City, and he wrote them nightly since coming, about the same time that Samuel did, to The Water's Edge Inn. He could talk a little more, but he's better than a chattering mouse I guess, Samuel sometimes thought.

Michael had re-entered the room after taking his morning piss. "It's wet out there, wet and hot already. Yuh think we'll still see fireworks?" He went to the corner of the room and pulled a shirt from his stack of clean laundry.

Samuel stood up and pulled his suspenders over his shoulders. The little that Michael Truman had said in the last three or four days had pertained only to the fireworks display set for that night. Samuel did not quite understand the obsession, or even try to, he just accepted it. "Don't worry Mikey, you'll get your fireworks. Christ, the sun is hardly up, the sky's got all day to clear," he gave his friend a pat on the back and headed out the door, "and it *will* clear up."

Michael Truman watched his roommate head down the stairs of the two-story and turn down the hall. He pulled his shirt on and shoved the window open. Sprigs of water hit his face and through the haze he saw his new friend crossing toward the stable. "You're sure about that, Samuel Flint!" he shouted.

Samuel turned to see the half-dressed stableboy leaning out their window. He continued walking, facing him, and yelled up, "I'm sure of it, Michael Truman. I'd bet my balls on it. Sit tight, you'll see, Mikey."

With that, Michael Truman's eyes danced. He watched Samuel disappear into the draping mists of white. "I hope you're right. Because I wanna see those fireworks tonight," he said quietly and shut the window.

Samuel walked down the path to the cow pasture. There, three short and squatty brown Guernseys—providers of enough cream and milk for Pottash's coffee and tea and, possibly, some eclairs or other dessert, for another day—

tucked themselves under the coolness of a motherly elm and waited, quite indifferently, for escort.

Mikey was right, he thought as he crossed onto the grass where the cows grazed each day shortly after he milked them. His shirt was already sticking to his chest and his back from the muggy heat, and the portion of his stocking that was exposed to the wet grass through the small hole in his left boot had become moist.

Hot, wet...and the mountains, barely visible from the clumps of vapor that hung low to the ground. Still, Samuel could make out their bold, stone-ish faces. Green tops of tall pines appeared to be trunkless and the soft sharp needles dripped with water and strong scent. Starlings bathed in a small puddle and chitchatted as he passed by.

Samuel Flint's "Whaaaaaa-whoooooooooo!!" echoed off the sides of the mountains that surrounded The Water's Edge Inn as he raised open hands to the sky.

The July sun soon ate its way through the gray overcoat and its rays licked up the excess water that last night's rainstorm had dumped on Pottash's little community. By noon, sitting high in the sky, the afternoon's paramour had seduced The Water's Edge Inn guests, as well. The back lawn became a tide of plaid cotton blankets and packed picnic baskets. Guests, as doubtful as Michael Truman had been that morning and as unfamiliar as him in matters of whimsical weather patterns in the Adirondacks, now sat in the sun, drinking expensive spirits and feeding each other grapes and cheese and bread from one another's basket. Pottash provided the gala with a roaming barbershop quartet and had promised a divine fireworks display accompanied by a ten-piece string orchestra.

While crossing the shrubbery early that afternoon, Samuel Flint had to smile inside as he saw some of the guests occasionally inspect their suit pants for a grass stain or brush their flowing and frilled dresses for a stray blade of grass that may have stuck. They are rolling in the dirt the best they know how, he thought.

The morning ritual of milking and feeding and turning the animals out to graze, and cleaning the stalls and exercising the horses, and bedding their stables, as well, took nearly until one o'clock. And Miss Stewart had asked him if he would, perhaps, milk and bottle one more crate later that afternoon, as she wished to whip the cream to top her dozen or so blueberry pies that she herself was personally baking for the festivities.

Samuel had, of course, agreed, and as the party and music and laughter continued, he retrieved one of the Guernseys from her spot in the shade. She unwillingly rose, and Samuel coaxed her back to her stall, nearly a half mile from where she rested with the other milkers.

Samuel squeezed another bucket of rich milk from her udder and dipped it into the bottles with which Miss Stewart had provided him. He let the milk set momentarily, however, and, sympathizing with the sweating cow he now called Gertie, walked her back to the pasture—and to her elm.

He then returned to the barn and heaved the crate on his left shoulder and set out for the Water's Edge kitchen, in aid of Miss Eliza Stewart's baking frenzy. Rather than cutting diagonally across the lawn and stepping here and there between the sprawled blankets and guests, today, Samuel hung back towards the shrubbery, reaching its end and squaring the corner that was closest to the kitchen.

Between this far end of the immaculately trimmed bush and the kitchen door, lie Pottash's orchard and berry patches. The apple trees in full blossom and with tiny fruits just forming shared their ground with pear and peach trees. All seemed adorned with interspersed shadows and shade and light.

"Yankee Doodle" had been stuck in Samuel's head since his waking—and he blamed, without mind, his roommate's eagered patriotism for the song's uninvited stay in his thought.

He whistled, and walked purposefully with his usual

long step. In no time, he passed the midway of the familiar trees...and without any intention really, turned his head into them for a look.

"'I've got a Yankee Doodle...'" His tune dwindled. He looked carefully, slowing his feet but still moving forward.

Perhaps what he saw a hundred yards in was a deer. He halted with that notion, his load still on his shoulder. A guess negated, as he then saw the hues of blue.

Perhaps a couple of blue herons had found their way into the trees. A tingle shot from spine to brain, and an anxious boy all over again, he remembered the last time he had seen one—it had been years since—

His eyes rose above the trickery of light and dark, wrestling a quick win over thought, and he was forced to dismiss his domino effect of idea.

Against the trunk of a fruit tree sat a young woman dressed in a light blue dress with a high lacey collar and flouncing trim. Her skirt descended with appropriate hug from her waist and, with her knees positioned as were and tucked to her chest, it reached only to just above her ankles. Samuel could make out the narrow strip of her black stockings between hem and boot. He reigned his strayed eyes back. In her hands, she held a small book. The sun cast streaks of white light through the branches and across her face and body and book, making, Samuel thought, her reading a bit difficult.

Still, he studied the scrutiny of her face, her squinting eyes on the words she read, and surmised that her world, at that moment, existed in the bound pages. He swayed where he stood, believing the scent of her perfume had reached his nostrils. He stepped towards—

"Flint! Flint!"

Samuel turned towards the kitchen where Miss Stewart stood in the open door with her hands cupped around her mouth and yelling his name.

"What the hell yuh waitin' for Samuel?" she questioned as he came closer.

"I thought you wanted me to pick the berries too, Miss

Eliza," he answered, although knowing that her question really hadn't required a response.

Her red, sweaty face revealed that she had labored hard over her pies and was in no mood for antics, so Samuel unloaded the milk and volunteered to beat the cream for her. Together they divided the bottles up and began to beat bowls of Gertie's soft thick fluid.

Cornelia McRamsee clutched the small book she had held when she heard a loud voice over the laughs and talk and singing of the gathering just beyond the orchard's edge. On looking up, she had seen a figure move away. Was her mother beckoning her? Surely that was the frame of a young man, though, and the voice was further off than that.

"Very well," she voiced aloud though no other human was near. Looking at her book, she closed it and directed her words to it, "You shall have to wait—again, and I shall return to the lawn with my fellow…my fellow…socialites." She laughed at the absurdity of it and left the orchard.

"Bargained for more than you thought, didn't yuh, Sammy?" Miss Eliza Stewart was bent over her last bowl of cream, giving it its last whooping.

Samuel was finishing his last, as well, and nearly an hour had passed since the two had set to the task. Both were drenched in sweat, Samuel more sopped under the arm, however, than Miss Eliza who was used to the heat and hard work in the confined space of a resort kitchen. Samuel gave his mound of cream one more quick spin with his beaters and shoved the bowl forward. He breathed hard and wiped the sweat off his forehead with his forearm, "I'll take the hot sun bakin' my back any day to workin' in this oven. Better yet, I could show yuh the pleasure in pullin' a cow's teat tomorrow mornin', Miss Eliza, bright and early, if yuh like."

"The hell you will, Flint! Don't be starin' at pretty girls in the orchard and you won't be gettin' yourself into messes like this again."

She rolled a laugh from her big belly and poked him with her elbow. She had seen the young McRamsee girl leave the orchard as Samuel was coming through the kitchen door.

They laughed a short time and Samuel bade, "Have a fine Fourth of July, Miss Stewart" as he picked up his crate full of empty bottles. Eliza was already spreading one of the bowls of cream on a pie.

"Hold yourself a second, Samuel." She wiped her hands on her apron and moved to the back of the kitchen where she opened a cabinet door and pulled something out and discreetly hid it behind her.

Samuel stood at the door, crate already on shoulder, and not knowing what she brought forth, still had an idea it was for him. "That won't be necessary, Ma'am."

"Ohhhh, don't you be tellin' me what is and isn't necessary, Mr. Flint." She winked and slipped a small bottle of tanned liquid into his pants pocket. Whiskey. Samuel smiled. "Enjoy the fireworks tonight, Samuel—and don't say you got it from me."

Samuel made his way back across the lawn, staying close to the route he had used earlier. The young girl had left her orchard, as he turned his head and searched the space for her. She now sat somewhere on one of those blankets, enjoying the wooing of a rich, handsome man, Samuel was sure. When in truth, Cornelia McRamsee had returned to her charcoal-gray blanket where she and her parents sat and listened to the potential profits of lumbering the trees of this very area. "Drive out the Goddamn mountain natives, or put them to work," Nathaniel Gorestone lectured as he poured another bottle of brandy for himself and his gentlemen listeners.

Samuel had reached the furthest end of the lawn,

fancying that his trek there was somewhat like walking the ebb of a human tide. He readied to turn into the opening of the shrubbery......

A photographer stood on the third floor balcony of The Water's Edge Inn and from his position he looked over the celebrating mass on the slightly inclining lawn below him. He stepped behind his tripodded apparatus and viewed his subjects through lens. Pottash would want each of his guests to have one, a real keeper, the photographer thought, then mentally added, who gives a shit—I'm getting paid for it. He snapped the button.

The frame before him froze, turning into blacks and grays and whites, a border around it......

Connie handed the photograph to her great-grandson. "What about MaryAnn, Matthew? Don't you hear from her?"

With photo in hand, Matthew moved from beside his great-grandmother's chair to the edge of the bed, where Samantha had been sitting earlier. He stared down at the picture. "No, Gram. I don't. I don't think I want to."

"What about the first time you saw her?"

"...I was sitting towards the back of this big lecture room. American Literature One—yuh know, Whitman, Thoureau, Emerson, and some of those realist guys. This girl came down the steps, came bouncing down the steps past me and I fell in love with the patches on her jeans, and her hair—it wasn't even her being beautiful—but I just remember being...drawn to her." He leaned forward some and handed the picture back to her. "Tell me more about this. Were there fireworks?"

Connie accepted the photograph and Matthew's answer. "Don't forget what that felt like, Matthew. Maybe you'll never feel it again the same way. So don't forget that—and, yes, there were fireworks..."

◆❖◆

Daylight had transformed into lucid darkness. Flashes of color, gold and red and green and blue, erupted above the treetops as Samuel hoisted himself from the porch roof outside his room window onto the larger, angular roof of the building. Michael Truman stood mesmerized from inside their room and quickly crawled out as he saw the lower body of his friend dangling and squirming upward. "Hurry, Sam. They've started."

Samuel looked over his shoulder to see the fading lights of the first big boom and gave himself a final push onto the higher roof. Seconds later, he was reaching down and pulling Michael up beside him. They seated themselves and could hear Pottash's orchestra in the distance as it vibrated Beethoven's Ninth into the Adirondacks. The long whizzz of a second episode of lights shortly muffled the music, and they watched and listened as the heavy crack of the rising specks of fuses turned into vibrant outpourings of colors.

"Not bad seats, aye, Truman?" Samuel nudged his comrade and passed the open bottle of whiskey from which he had already swigged.

From the rooftop, the two young men could see the display without obstruction and beyond the shrubbery, to the back lawn where the fireworks cast light and shadow over The Water's Edge Inn guests, as well.

The descending light's glow streaked across Michael's face. He accepted the bottle, not turning until the last color faded. Tipping it, he sipped and drew his head back from the strong burning, as the liquid trailed off down to his gut. "First class, Samuel." He took another small gulp of the whiskey and passed it back.

The two sat in silence as the display continued, and Samuel watched it all, the bright lights, the endless sky and the lawn and the people there, as their sounds of awe could be heard from where he sat. And he glimpsed at Michael Truman's face as the almost-man-turned-complete-child stared at the sight before him with his mouth gaping just a little.

...They sat, their eyes absorbed, their mouths and bodies imbibed. An ample share of Miss Stewart's generous gift washed down, as if a round passed celebrated each brief portion of the lighted pageant...

"You do love them, don't you Mikey?"

"I do," he said, "...they fly up and light the sky for beauty—and beauty alone—for the people that watch them and then, in seconds, they are gone, their life is over." He shrugged and made to get up.

"Wait. There'll be a finale." Samuel took his hand and blocked Michael's movement. "And you don't say much, Michael Truman, but when you do, you say it right. Maybe you should write some of that stuff in those letters you're sendin' home, you might have yourself a book someday."

The drink unharnessed Michael's tongue further, and his replying at all surprised himself, "Yuh think?"

Samuel patted Michael's back. "Hells yeah, I think."

"Ode to Joy" floated towards them and in the heart of it, ten or more loud whirling whistles followed one after the other and exploded into shimmering globes of blues and silvers and greens...

Cornelia McRamsee swore she felt the blood pulsating through her heart and her fingertips, as she watched and listened until the last blisters of spark popped and faded. The brief light illuminated the trees' bodies and the mountains' faces, and her eyes wandered beyond her realm...and into theirs.

Chapter Seven

He turned his head from his work at hand and spat a gob of brownish juice into the hay onto the stable floor.

"That, sir, is *simply* nasty."

The voice behind him passed a ripple of startle through his body. He made one more long sweep with brush in hand down the horse's back and across its rump, and turned around. A shade of pink rose through his face from being caught chewing tobacco on the sacred grounds of The Water's Edge Inn by a woman guest, but especially by one as beautiful as she who stood before him.

Tobacco was a luxury he could not afford and, therefore, bummed it from one of the other livery hands to enjoy on his hours off duty. He knew Miss Stewart would not kindly look upon it if he were found out, but, rather than worrying about being ratted on, he mostly hoped this young lady, one whom he immediately recognized, did not see his reddened cheek. He hated to be caught off guard, and he thought that, perhaps, the dimness of the barn would hide his look.

She stood in the doorframe, and the afternoon sun streamed through an open window and cast across her. Hair, dark and wavy, fell on her shoulders and cupped her defined face. She had pulled some locks back and clasped them with a shining white barrette decorated with pearls. He hesitated slightly, lost in her milky skin and unharnessed hazel eyes. "The stables are closed, Miss. For the afternoon. Perhaps, you can ride tomorrow?" He stepped away from the horse, placed the brush on the windowsill, and moved closer to Cornelia.

Listening to his words, she reached into her velvet satchel. She had only seen the outline of a young man spitting a few moments earlier and, until he had stepped forward into the light of the window, she had not realized it was the young man she had seen, or admired, a few days earlier. She removed her eyes from him and nearly dropped her bag as she pulled out a silver and gold cigarette case. "Oh, hello. Or rather, well, that just won't do," she said, opening the case and returning her eyes to him.

"Not in here, Miss," he pointed behind him, "not with all this hay lying around." He reached toward her and snapped her case shut. "Fancy little thing just to carry your smokes around, isn't it?" he asked.

Both laughed then, an air of awkwardness broken. "Won't you join me outside for one then?" she offered. "I would so like to make arrangements to ride."

"It'd be my pleasure, Miss…"

"Miss McRamsee. Mr…" She raised her eyebrows in question.

"Flint," he answered. "We'll move some from the barn and have us a smoke." He spit his quid out and ran his tongue between his bottom teeth and lip, and spit again onto a small pile of horse shit.

Cornelia followed him then, as he led her out of the back entrance of the stable barn, away from the main buildings of The Water's Edge Inn.

They walked past the corral that jutted out from one side of the rather broad barn that was used for the horses, and that encompassed a grand patch of thick green grass. In it, forty or more horses of all hues and breeds grazed. One, in particular, immediately entranced Cornelia. The muscles of its legs, the arch of its back, the slow swishing of its tail, and twitch of its tan ears. An appaloosa with a spotted rump.

Walking beside Cornelia, Mr. Flint had followed the gaze of her eyes to the horse in the far right of the pasture. "You like her?" he asked.

"Yes. Yes, I do. She is so graceful just standing there eating and persuading the flies to let her be that I can't imagine what it would be like to ride her."

"She is beautiful. I haven't had the chance to open her up just yet. Do you ride?"

They continued walking, past the corral, and up a small bridle path with maples and oaks on either side.

"Yes, well, not exactly—that is why I ventured down to the stables because I am anxious to learn."

"Then maybe you can have the honors. After you learn, of course." Mr. Flint led Cornelia to the end of the path, a path halting suddenly at a clearing and a wide pond that seemed to have…*landed*…in the middle of this wooded area behind The Water's Edge, behind the stable and the corral. Some wild ducks flapped the surface and flew, surprised at the visitors disturbing their afternoon swim and meal of minnows.

Cornelia thought, for a second, about two days earlier and of Robert Stimes. "How absolutely magnificent," she said and reopened her small case. She removed a cigarette and delayed placing it between her lips, "You don't mind if I don't use a cigarette-holder, do you, Mr. Flint?" She passed the opened miniature coffer to the young man.

His face expressed nonchalance. "Fine by me," he said and took a cigarette, as well, and a match and struck the latter on the hard etched surface of the shiny box. He lit Cornelia and then himself, and handed the closed case back to her. "Thank you, Miss McRamsee. Shall we sit?" He flung the match into the pond and motioned to the edge of the water where a few rocks sat.

Both found a place and did not speak for a minute or two. They dragged on their cigarettes and soaked the reflection of the sun off from the pond's surface. The ducks had circled back and landed on the further end of the water.

"Open her up? How do you mean?"

Samuel tilted his head. "Hmm?"

"You said earlier that you hadn't had the chance to open that appaloosa up and that maybe I might have that honor."

"Oh. Yeah, open her up." He smiled broadly. "You see it's one thing to ride a horse, like when one of the boys takes a group on one of those excursions they do here every morning. You wind around on some of the trails, and it's a nice thing to do an' all in itself. But, if you really want to ride, you take one of these animals out to an open field or valley and give her just a quick nudge with your feet behind her ribs," he used his hands to point to this area of the horse, as if it stood in front of him, "let her have the reins, and just let her fly. That's what I mean by openin' her up. You can't beat it, it's like—you're in control and you're not. You've got wings. Yuh see?"

She looked back across the pond and watched a glittering green-headed mallard bob its head beneath the surface. She smiled. "Yes, I see."

They smoked for a few more moments.

"Can you show me? Teach me to ride? I don't want a trail ride, I want to ride as you speak of it." There, she thought, I have said it.

Samuel thought of how engrossed Miss McRamsee was in the book she had been reading when he had seen her the other day. "Nothing's free, Miss McRamsee."

Cornelia scowled and began to rise.

"Now hold on one second, Miss, sure, yeah, I'll teach you to ride, but it has to be when I ain't workin' and—" he paused, "—and I don't get the chance to get my hands on many good books and the other day you looked like you were really eatin' up what you were readin'."

"You want to read my book…in exchange for riding instruction? Of course, yes, yes—"

"I may need a translation to go along with it from time to time, if you—"

"Why, yes, Mr. Flint. Certainly, we have a deal."

Cornelia reached out to him. Realizing she still held her cigarette in her outstretched hand, she smiled and laughed. She tossed it in the pond, and Samuel took one more drag on his and did the same.

They shook hands and Samuel helped Cornelia to her feet. She straightened her dress and they headed back down the path to the grounds of The Water's Edge Inn.

Chapter Eight

Had it been a highly traveled road, the dust from passing cars or carriages would have risen from it and sojourned to the teacups and full dinner plates of those who took their lunch on the edge of the front lawn of The Water's Edge Inn. Tables had been set close to the road, for not further than twenty feet on the opposite side lay Blue Heron Lake.

Several guests roamed its shores, some anxious to learn to canoe or sail, others insisting that the air was cooler coming off from it. Most, however, did not realize that they were drawn to it for its simple beauty. Its width, covering more than two miles, ended abruptly as its furthest side was seemingly stopped by the mountain range rolling past. And as the sun squatted high above the resort, it captured the mountains' image and tossed it upon the lake.

Cornelia had heard the head servant tell one of the guests that, before Pottash had begun construction, herons commonly waded his shallow end of the lake, hence the name came. Plume hunters chased them out too—the woman had slyly added, as if she shouldn't divulge that information—lucky to see one in these parts, being they're humble birds, to boot.

Cornelia tried to imagine the likes of these lanky birds standing about in the water before her, and wondered if she would recognize one if she saw it.

"Henry tells me you'll be unpacking your bags for good this fall, Mr. Stimes." Mrs. McRamsee had arranged for her and her daughter to take lunch with Robert Stimes, and Mrs. Lawrence had joined them, as well. The four sat at the round table and drank a lukewarm after-dinner tea.

"Oh, how grand, Mr. Stimes. Perhaps, some place in our area? Our growing city needs a man like you." Mrs. Lawrence held her saucer and teacup in her hands, and acted startled at news she had heard days earlier on the way to The Water's Edge Inn.

"Why, yes. Actually, I am thinking of paying someone to do my gold digging for me now, ladies, and am ready to settle in a lovely home on the outskirts of Albany." Stimes had purchased a three-story mansion about ten miles west of the city and his people were filling it with his worldly possessions as he sat in conquest with the only other object he wished to bring there. "Perhaps, you could do a painting or two for my new study, Miss McRamsee. Your mother mentioned your fine ability with watercolor."

"Yes, perhaps, Mr. Stimes." Cornelia nodded to the servant boy as he refilled her cup, and she concealed her shock at the disclosure of Stimes's new residence that was less than an hour's travel west of the McRamsee estate in Albany. "However, my mother is too generous in her descriptions, I assure you."

The servant made his way around to each of the guests at the table and replenished their drink, and the conversation floundered like a mackerel just drawn out of water and slapped onto a boat's deck.

"What is it young ladies your age read, Cornelia? How you do love to read, as well." Mrs. McRamsee pounced on the possibility-turned-impossibility of a brewing discourse between the two youngest people seated.

Cornelia had played this game of bat and ball too often with her mother. "Mother, I am sure Mr. Stimes and Mrs. Lawrence care little—"

"Nonsense, Cornelia. We would love to hear. Don't you agree, Mrs. Lawrence?" Stimes looked across the table.

Mary Francis nodded in agreement. "Oh, yes, Cornelia. You must share with us what is in that brown book that I have seen you take out from time to time."

"It is *Leaves of Grass*, Mrs. Lawrence, by an American poet named Walt Whitman." She did not retrieve the book from her satchel, but smiled socially instead.

"Now that does sound familiar, Cornelia." Mrs. Lawrence turned her head towards the water as if it would somehow clear a street in her memory.

"Won't you quote something, Cornelia. Do you find inspiration in it for your artwork?" Stimes had leaned forward slightly.

This will do just fine, Mrs. McRamsee thought and ripped the hook from the bleeding mouth of the mackerel and threw the fish back into the sea.

The book remained in Cornelia's bag. "Very well, if you insist.

"I am the poet of the Body and I am the poet of
the Soul,
The pleasures of heaven are with me and the
pains of hell are with me,

The first I graft and increase upon myself, the
latter I translate into a new tongue.

I am the poet of woman the same as the man,
And I say it is as great to be a woman as to be a
man."

"Oh my word." Mary Francis sat up straight in her chair and ran her hands twice down the lap of her dress.

Mrs. McRamsee said nothing and glanced her eyes toward Robert Stimes.

"My dear Cornelia," Stimes started with, and sat back in his chair. His words ceased as his eyebrows lifted and amusement blurted from his gut to his open mouth. His laughter halted only as air journeyed downward when necessary. He reminded Cornelia of a schoolboy about to piss his pants over a prank played on the headmaster.

"I have offended you, Mrs. Lawrence. And I have...delighted you, Mr. Stimes. If you will excuse me." Cornelia slid her chair back.

"Cornelia. You will sit." Mrs. McRamsee reached for her daughter's arm.

"Yes, now I know where I have heard of Mr. Whitman and his writing—our Father Martin, during a service some years ago, warned—"

Cornelia's mother's hand moved too late, and Cornelia stood. "Yes, *warned* you, Mrs. Lawrence, I am sure, of the poet's undeniable equating of the heaven-bound soul with the human body." She turned and headed towards the inn.

"Cornelia. Cornelia." Mrs. McRamsee had stood, as well. "I do apologize. Mr. Stimes. Mrs. Lawrence."

"Quite all right, Mrs. McRamsee. Sit, sit." Mr. Stimes had regained his composure to an extent, although a blurt of laughter still shot from his mouth as he persuaded the woman back into her seat. "She is a young girl, and Mrs. Lawrence and I understand her...impetuous nature. Right, Mrs. Lawrence?"

If Robert Stimes was letting the incident pass, she would also. "Not to worry, Julia, she will come around."

Cornelia McRamsee could hear the voices of other guests sitting scattered across the lawn and they warbled the sounds of the excuses being proposed at the table she had just left.

"I suppose you are right. Even so, Henry and I will have to have a talk with our Cornelia."

The three signaled the servant for another tray of crumpets and continued their afternoon.

Cornelia had asked a timid young man tending to the horses in the corral where Mr. Flint might be, and he had pointed to another small stable, behind the larger one and the cow barn, where tack and saddles were kept. "That way, Miss, I believe he just went behind that there building."

A few moments later, having followed the edge of the corral, Cornelia stepped towards the back of the building that sat close to a strip of woods. She paused briefly at the sound of…she wasn't sure. A trickling stream of water on wood? "Mr. Flint?" she voiced and rounded the corner.

Samuel stood facing the backside of the tack house and turned a degree away from the eyes of Miss McRamsee. He looked over his shoulder and could not help but grin. "You do have a knack for walkin' in on me at the most awkward times, Miss McRamsee."

Cornelia retraced her step back around the corner and leaned against the wall. She attempted to press her lips as they too could not help but form a smirk. "There are facilities for that, Mr. Flint."

Samuel had finished and was behind her shoulder now, and leaning with his arm stretched up the corner. "All the same, Miss McRamsee, all the same. You're right on time, I just got off. And, please, it's Samuel—if'an you don't mind."

They stood facing each other, only a few inches apart, as Cornelia had turned towards him. "Very well…Samuel."

She faltered with word, taking a step back. "How shall we begin?"

"I thought first we might get the basics down, Miss McRamsee. I'll show you a bridle or two in here and grab you a saddle. No better way to learn than to get on and ride."

They walked to the open end of the tack shed where at least a hundred different bridles hung on both sides of the longer walls of the building. The back wall and upper floor, reachable by the ladder propped in the middle of the ground and extending into a cutout hole, housed the Western and English saddles. The whole space smelled of horse and leather.

Samuel did his best explaining some of the bridles, the more expensive and extravagant ones, but after he returned from the left corner with a worn-in one, he assured Cornelia, "A horse doesn't know how much you paid for one of those. She wants one that feels right, that gives her as much play as she can possibly have." He let her hold the darkened reins as he worked his way with his hands down to the bit and took hold of the shiny piece of curved metal. "This here we'll slide into the horse's mouth, and with the touch of the reigns on her face and the tug in her mouth, she'll know which way you want her to go." He demonstrated, using his hand as the horse's mouth.

"It looks rather uncomfortable to be sticking in a horse's mouth, Mr.—Samuel."

Samuel watched Cornelia's nose crinkle in doubt. "I agree, Miss McRamsee—if we used, say, somethin' like this." He went over to the wall and pulled down a bridle. The bit was angled like a triangle with a sharp peak. "Yuh see, this bit, well, the horse will sure as hell—pardon my language an' all—but she'll know that thing is pokin' in the tender of her mouth, and with the one you got, well, she's used to it and it's like us havin' a piece of straw tucked in ours. The less that horse knows you're up there, in my humblest opinion, Miss McRamsee, the better she'll ride you. And the better you'll ride yourself." He winked then.

"And besides, the bridle you're holdin' is used by the best."

"And that would be?"

"Yours truly, Miss McRamsee. Let's get you on that horse."

Cornelia's appaloosa approached the two as they made their way to her. Samuel withdrew a sugar cube from his pocket and handed it to Cornelia. "Meet your new friend, Miss McRamsee."

"Please. Cornelia—or Connie, rather, if you like."

"OK—Connie. Keep your hand and fingers flat out when you feed her so she doesn't take a bite outa yuh."

Connie followed Samuel's instructions and placed the sugar cube in the center of her flat palm. The appaloosa hoofed closer and sniffed, its wet, warm, and whiskered nose-lips fumbling and strangely tickling Connie's hand.

As the mare found the cube, Samuel moved forward and slipped the bridle over her head and ears, and worked the bit into her mouth, and she, of course, stepped back and threw her head in gentle protest. Samuel handed the reins to Cornelia. "We'll lead her out the back of the corral and set you atop of her."

"Samuel, what about a saddle?" Cornelia led the horse as Samuel walked on the other side of it. "Surely, I can't ride this—her—without a saddle?"

"I got a feelin' about you Cornelia McRamsee and somethin' tells me you can."

They walked past a few of the other horses scattered in the fenced pasture. The animals' heads rose and then returned to their grazing. Samuel opened the back gate and Cornelia led the horse out and waited for him to close the latch behind them. Trees separated ahead as a bridle path, half the width of a road, stretched and wound into them.

They walked the horse, anxious and agreeable for exercise, a bit further. "All right, then, do you feel ready?" Samuel halted the small party and rubbed the appaloosa under her chin.

"I believe I am." Connie looked into the horse's eye. "Are you?" she asked it and looked at Samuel and moved to the side he stood on.

Mounting seemed easy, as Samuel flipped the horse's reins over its head, and boosted Connie, with his hands on her hips, onto the animal's back.

Connie sat, her legs dangling on the side of the horse and her hands on Samuel's shoulders. "Auh," she grunted or giggled as her buttocks met the horse's arch. "Samuel?" she asked in guidance.

"Connie, you'll want to swing your right leg over her." He moved his hands to the bottom of her left boot to brace her. The horse began to step some.

Cornelia was silently thankful that she had not worn one of her fanciful event or evening dresses with narrow bottom hem as her mother had suggested she might for their lunch date with Mr. Stimes, still, even in this day dress with its little looser fit at feet—"Samuel, I'm not sure."

"Miss McRamsee, you are sure. Now stop thinkin' and just do what comes natural."

With that, Connie shifted her body and lifted the necessary length of skirt that she felt material and make did not allow for mobility, and swung her right leg over the horse and then grabbed the reins.

A quick mental inventory suddenly seized her and she deemed what dresses could, would be worn on future excurs—

A short inner-embarrassment and a fear of jinxing the hopeful hampered her in mid-thought.

"I do believe you're about to ride your first horse, Connie. Am I right?"

Somewhat relieved Samuel's words did not indicate he had heard her mind's conversation, Connie smiled and glanced down at the reins in her hands, and then looked towards her new instructor. "You are right, Samuel Flint."

Samuel took the left rein, held it, and walked beside Connie and the horse until he was absolutely sure both were suited for each other. They walked for nearly a mile this way, with Samuel's hand on the rein and Connie learning how to maneuver the animal this way or that. The horse paid little heed when Samuel removed his hand and Connie was in complete control, and the three of them strolled deeper into the woods until the path looped around and headed back for the gate.

Though the trail twisted through a canopy constructed from the arms of tall pines and ash and alder and the like, the air remained warm as the summer sun stretched through every opening it could find. The young man and woman and animal were so remote from The Water's Edge Inn or anywhere, really, that all they could hear was the clump clump of the horse's hooves and the easy pace of Samuel's feet on the dry ground.

Cornelia absorbed the rugged bark of the oaks that she passed and the shell-like coating of the white birch and the clear glow of the sun's rays as they crept by the branches and directly hit the forest floor. She looked occasionally at the young man beside her, as well, and watched how he too looked up and around, but never down, and seemed to smile (though she could only see his profile at times) when a bird whistled or a rabbit darted further in the wood from its supposed foe. She noticed his steadying of the horse with his one hand when necessary, and his long stride beside her.

A periodical snort of the appaloosa brought Cornelia's attention away from a treetop nest she had been studying, and she looked down to Samuel.

A trickle of sweat wiggled down the side of his face and sat to rest on his jaw.

"My Lord, Samuel, I am sorry. Here, I have been riding for over an hour, or nearly two, and you have walked the whole way. Do let me get down and let you ride for a bit."

Samuel had not been oblivious to the presence of this young woman on the horse beside him. He, too, had glanced up at her, without her noticing, and watched her explore his world. He liked the fragrance of her perfume and its mingling with the horse's sweat and the pines. Yes, he had been quite aware of her presence, but, even still, her voice after the long silence…

"I'm fine, Connie," he said and looked toward her left boot and its pointed heel. "Besides, it doesn't appear you've brought your walkin' shoes."

Connie, too, looked at her feet. "No, I don't suppose I have, Samuel…but I would insist that, well, perhaps, we both could ride—that is if you don't mind, girl." She put her face close to the horse's and patted its neck. Pulling the reins, she halted the whole procession.

Samuel admired how quickly she had learned. He looked up at her. "Won't be necessary, Con—"

"I won't take no for an answer, Samuel Flint," she said, extending her hand to him and bracing herself a little with her right, as if ready to pull him up.

No less than a half-hour earlier, Samuel had felt the formation of a small blister starting on his left little toe. Without another word, he rounded Connie's wrist with his hand and jumped and swung himself up and behind the young woman.

"Careful what you ask for Miss Cornelia McRamsee," he said, placing his arms around her waist and giving the horse a small jab beneath its ribs with his feet.

"Shall I show you how it's done." She lifted the reins a little higher, as if riding in a show ring. "Hold tightly, now." She then gave the animal a foot poke of her own and they began to gallop at a little faster pace.

"You do think you can ride a horse now, don't yuh?" Cornelia heard in her left ear, as she kept eyes on the path.

She turned her head slightly, and, on her ear, she could feel his breath. "I don't *think*—I do what comes naturally."

Samuel tightened his arms around her waist a notch…approvingly.

Samuel slid down from the horse and then helped Cornelia in dismount when they reached the back gate of the corral. "Not bad, Connie. Not bad at all."

Cornelia contrived a look of shock. "Not bad? Not bad? That was a grand ride and you must admit it," she professed, whacking Samuel with the horse's reins.

"Oww, oww. All right, all right, it waaas...pretty grand, Miss Connie. Pretty grand, indeed. You'll be ready for an open field sooner than I thought."

They made plans to do some reading and to meet the next day, perhaps a little earlier if Samuel could get his chores done...

...While on the opposite end of the corral, between the back legs of a patient filly, Timothy Wemple had abruptly knelt. There, he doctored a joint that needed no such attention and sat watching that Flint character and a real good-lookin' woman since he had first seen the two emerge from the woods together a few minutes earlier. He stretched his neck a bit more so he could—CRACK—the horse's cordial composure turned spooked and her hoof found the tender of two testicles. "Son of a bitch!" Timothy Wemple rolled to the ground and cupped his throbbing, already-swelling reward.

Chapter Nine

Though the hour was five in the afternoon, Connie climbed the stairs to the McRamsee second floor suite as if she were creeping in at three in the morning. Most of the guests were already in the huge dining room kiddy-corner to the breakfast room and on the opposite side of the resort. She heard the distant sounds of talk billowing out through its open, twelve-foot high mahogany doors, and had crossed the back lawn on the opposite side of the orchards and came around the front of The Water's Edge Inn, as she had expected the quietude that she now encountered.

Miss Eliza Stewart spent her afternoons, after busily pleasing Pottash's richly crew, as she had come to refer to them as such in her head, wiping down some of the woodwork and feather-dusting some of the mirrors that clung to the inn's walls. She exited the breakfast room, having cleaned around the brass doorknobs, and intended to give the staircase banister, with its grooves of majestic angels and clouds, a scrub-down.

Cornelia was halfway up the stairs when she heard the escalating sound of woman's whistling. She climbed two steps at a time, but she now heard "Oh, When the Saints" at the base of the ascension.

She stopped.

She turned slowly.

"Good afternoon, Miss McRamsee. How are you today?" Eliza bent on her knees to her work, and would get to the root of why the young girl looked like she had just hidden Pottash's nose hair trimmer, God knowing he needed one.

Cornelia descended a few stairs, recognized the head servant and quickly conjured up her name. "Good afternoon, Miss Stewart. Lovely day, isn't it?"

"For a ride, aye, Miss McRamsee." Eliza worked her cloth around the naked foot of one of the angels.

Both hands on the railing, Connie climbed closer to Miss Stewart. "I beg your pardon?" she said, having heard perfectly Eliza's words.

The woman kept her cloth moving, but glanced up. "I said that it was a lovely day for a horseback ride." She lifted her dust cloth to point at Cornelia's dress. "Pardon me, Miss, but you do have just a bit of soot or other stuff on the behind, or the back, of your dress."

Connie felt the rump of her dress, below the narrow of her back and where her buttocks had sat on the bare back of the horse, and her face reddened. She walked to the foot of the stairs where Miss Stewart polished, and bent beside her. "Is it—is it a noticeable marking—because, because, my mother has spent so much on this very dress, and I, or rather, she will be livid."

Eliza brought her cloth to her knees and looked at the flustered girl in front of her. "Miss, if you don't mind me sayin', I lived in these mountains long enough to know when someone's been ridin' a horse without a saddle by the sorta brownish mark you got on your butt, and if you really don't mind me sayin'..."

"Continue, please."

"You don't smell that fine either, and—and I think you like young Samuel Flint just as much or more than horses, Miss McRamsee."

"Miss Stewart—"

"I beggin' your pardon again, Miss McRamsee, and I know it is not in my place, but—"

Cornelia's flush face faded pale again almost as quickly as it had pinked, and she put her hand on Miss Stewart's hand, the one that held the dusting rag. "Miss Stewart, I ask that—"

Eliza rested the rag on her knee and turned her hand upward to cup the young woman's. "Miss McRamsee, you're about to ask me to launder your dress—personally launder it, ain't yuh?" She got to her knees and pulled herself erect with the help of the angelled banister. "Shall we head upstairs and get you out of it...while the others are dinin'?"

Together they climbed the stairs and entered the empty McRamsee suite. Behind the closed doors of Connie's room, Miss Eliza Stewart helped her out of her dress and corset. Connie scribbled her parents a note apologizing for missing dinner and saying that she did not feel well, and placed it on the desk by the suite's entrance. She returned to her room as the servant woman was bundling up the dress.

Connie slipped under her satin sheets and heard the exiting steps of her accomplice. They had not spoken since they had ascended the stairs.

"Miss Stewart..."

Eliza turned.

"Thank you."

"Is it worth it, Miss McRamsee?"

"It is."

"I thought so." She winked at the young girl whose

natural pale complexion had a touch of flavor from the sun, and then she closed the door behind her.

July nights in the Adirondacks pass like a child's infant years. They depend on the day and then grow from it, crawl and creep forward as the sun takes hours to set. And then dusk becomes dark, though that intermittent step barely exists, and, so, as the infant turns toddler, the night like she, never walks but runs from then on.

When the early morning sun passed light through Cornelia's window, she woke thinking she had only napped. Though she felt completely replenished, she still thought that yesterday's sun hadn't even set yet. She settled in the moment between asleep and awake, flashing images through her head.

Yesterday's ride…

…the tack house…

…her lunch on the front lawn, the white circular table with its fine china…

…the massive lake with the mountains in and behind it…

…the great blue heron flapping its huge wings as it left the water's edge—

As it rose and flew towards the blue stones, dream and wakefulness ceased their lovemaking and Cornelia opened her eyes. The incident with her mother and Mrs. Lawrence and Mr. Stimes washed over her consciousness. She rolled over in her bed and looked directly into her open window as the bright white of the sun's rays angled its threshold. Its warmth had dried the sudden flood and she found what she would do.

"Good morning, Mother."

Holding teacup in hand, Mrs. McRamsee turned on the

suite parlor's sofa to see her daughter entering. Cornelia came around the davenport and kissed her mother's cheek. A servant girl, the same one who had helped Cornelia into dress this morning, followed her in the room and prepared a tea for her.

Cornelia took a seat next to her mother and nodded to the servant as she was handed the tea. "Mother, I must start by say—"

"Cornelia, your father is hunting this morning with Robert Stimes. I do wish that he were here because we need to consider your future. Cornelia. We need to discuss with you, our daughter, what we both want for you...Yesterday's episode, Cornelia Margaret McRamsee, was appalling and embarrassing and will not occur again. Is that understood? Is that understood?"

"That is understood, Mother, and—"

"Your father will discuss matters with you when he finds the right moment. He will be returning shortly with Mr. Stimes, who will be joining us for breakfast. That will not be the right moment, so for the time, you are spared." Mrs. McRamsee took a deep breath. Her eyes protruded forward, on her daughter's face.

"I am sorry for my behavior yesterday, Mother. I do not know what came over me. I behaved on whim, and I apologize."

Julia McRamsee had not expected such immediate resignation from her daughter, but did not question it. "Very well, then, Cornelia."

They sat for some time, nearly three-quarters of an hour, drinking tea and stirring what remained in their cups. The clanking of spoons on the wet walls of the pale china played master to all other noise until the men came through the suite's door. The hollow tinging renounced reign to baritone laughter and boots clumping hard across the oak floor and merry words particular to the duck hunting that morning.

"Good morning, ladies," the men clucked as they entered the parlor. From behind the couch, Henry

McRamsee kissed his wife's cheek, and Mrs. McRamsee smelled the sweet scent of apricot brandy as it billowed from the cavity of his mouth. The two men took seats on the opposite side of the coffee table, in another sofa facing the women.

"We are sorry to say we will not be having any roast duck this afternoon." Stimes slapped Henry's leg, and both engaged in another cliquey round of laughter.

Mrs. McRamsee wondered.

Cornelia cared less.

"If Robert had gone about the business, by God, we would be having a feast, but, rather, he let me do the shooting and with each shot I took, and missed, he insisted we engage in a game that he and his brothers used to play back in Pennsylvania."

"For every shot ol' Henry took and then missed his mark, he did a shot of brandy. Now, by his sixth shot, I thought I should help him out, not with the gun, of course, but with the drink."

"How gentlemanly of you, Mr. Stimes," Cornelia began...and then barricaded her tongue. Her train must travel on a different track, she forced herself to remember, at least here, with those she sat. She smiled. "Now we shall go hungry this afternoon?"

The servant entered the room then, announcing breakfast, and the group moved into the suite's dining room. The lengthy table held toast and eggs and meats and juices, enough to feed a small English army.

The men continued talk of the ducks that Mr. McRamsee had missed, and Robert coached the older gentleman on how to hold and aim a gun and encouraged him on the attempts he had made and insisted they hunt in a much more serious fashion sometime soon. The women sat quietly and listened, Mrs. McRamsee asking the pertinent questions when applicable.

Nearly two hours had passed in this manner, and as Mr. Stimes pushed his chair back and removed his napkin from his lap, Mrs. McRamsee decided to check the train schedule of her daughter's new line. "Perhaps you could walk Cornelia down by the lake, Mr. Stimes, and convince her to paint you something for that new study of yours, after all." Mrs. McRamsee patted her mouth with the corner of the white napkin she held.

"Miss Cornelia?" Mr. Stimes looked across the table at the beautiful young woman.

She smiled and would stop at her parents' station.

"Convincing won't be necessary, Mother." She stood. "Allow me to gather my purse and my parasol and I will be right with you, Mr. Stimes."

"Definitely a landscape...and perhaps, a portrait, Miss Cornelia. Could you do a portrait of me?" Stimes's early morning buzz had completely faded as he walked along the lake's edge with Connie.

The sun headed for its noontime position, and Cornelia, even with her open parasol, basked in its heat and felt as if it were only a few miles off. "If you'd like, Mr. Stimes. Why not with you holding one of your guns or—"

"That's a wonderful idea. I shall stand in some Napoleonic fashion with that large rifle I used on the range the other day and, perhaps, I can have a kill in the other."

"What sort of other things do you shoot, Mr. Stimes."

Pebbles that had been pushed ashore from the depths of the lake in storm and wind kept the pair's shoes from sinking into the fertile ground beneath them.

"Everything and anything, Miss McRamsee. The bigger the better. I should like to kill one of these blue herons that are said to be around here."

"I believe they are quite rare, Mr. Stimes."

"One less will do no harm. Besides, I must say that the most rare and the most precious kill does something to one's heart, Miss McRamsee, it makes it beat faster and louder, I believe." Stimes fisted his hand and pounded it over his heart twice. "Yes, a sense of self emerges."

"I see" came quickly to Cornelia's lips. She had remembered to put *Leaves of Grass* in her satchel and had walked long enough with Mr. Robert Stimes.

They headed up the small embankment, across the road, and onto the front lawn of The Water's Edge Inn where servants were preparing tables with silverware and tablecloths.

"Would you care to join me for lunch, Cornelia?" Stimes asked as he glanced at a young couple seating themselves.

"If you will pardon me, Mr. Stimes, perhaps I will lie down for a short time before I eat, as the sun seems to have fatigued me. Do you mind much?" Connie took down her parasol and readied to part.

"Not at all. Dinner, perhaps?" Mr. Stimes bowed, and took and kissed Cornelia's hand.

"Yes, you may make arrangements with my parents, Mr. Stimes." She withdrew her extended arm and headed for the lobby of the resort.

Robert Stimes did not doubt Miss Cornelia McRamsee's new found sincerity; nevertheless, as she passed through the front doors of The Water's Edge, he wondered if she would climb the stairs to her family's suite for her nap.

He casually sauntered over to a table until she passed through the doors and then he changed his direction, moving towards the entrance through which Cornelia had just gone.

As Cornelia closed the door behind her, she turned her head slightly to watch Mr. Stimes make his way to a table on the front lawn. She quickly moved through the lobby and into the breakfast room where a few servants were cleaning up after the morning feast, then passed through the swinging doors of the kitchen and exited to the back lawn from there. Her intrusion into a staff premises went unnoticed for the most part, except for the head servant whose eyes met the young girl's, as Cornelia turned to close the screen door behind her. She stayed close to the orchard side of the back lawn and squared the corner, thinking that the dark green dress she wore somehow blended her with the shrubbery as she walked along it.

...Robert Stimes stood in the breakfast room in front of the wall of glass and watched as Cornelia McRamsee passed along the last ten feet of the shrubbery and turned into its opening, towards the stables and barns of The Water's Edge Inn.

Chapter Ten

Samuel splashed water over his face from the horses' trough in the corral. His work shirt stuck to his back from the racing around he had done that morning. Even though he had learned earlier on in life on his father's farm that, regardless of the hour that he woke or the pace that he moved during the day, work always had a way of taking the same length of time.

He had started his morning before the sun even began to glow behind the mountains, by getting the cows from the pasture, walking them into the barn, milking them. The daily morning ritual. He cleaned and hayed the horses and had gained some time, but in the process had noticed that a young colt, a stark black thoroughbred, walked this morning with a limp. Upon examination, he found that the animal had somehow, perhaps on a jagged stone, chipped a rather large clip out of her front hoof and loosened her shoe, and that this mischance had rendered her lameness. Samuel didn't think twice about corralling the uncooperating fiend into a tight pen where he could crawl in beside her, rope her leg up, and shave any of the broken hoof down and retighten her shoe; however, the whole procedure is more quickly written of than accomplished.

For all the sweat, he had only finished no more than a

quarter of an hour earlier with his chores than usual. He had bridled up the appaloosa and a horse he liked to call his own, a feisty mare with a creamed coffee coat and dark chocolate mane and tail. Their reins extended to a post next to the back gate.

He waited at the front gate, closest to the shrubbery, for Connie McRamsee, and then would walk her around the corral to the horses and take her to the further end of the pond that they had sat by the other day.

"Whatcha doin' Flint?" Timothy Wemple carried a pitchfork between barn and stables when he saw Samuel leaning against a top corral board and looking towards the far end of the shrubbery. The inquirer's greasy red hair stuck to his forehead.

Wemple had been assigned head stableman upon his arrival at The Water's Edge Inn more for the fact that he was the oldest of the young men who would work there and that he was probably the first to apply for the position, before the hiring was in Miss Eliza Stewart's hands, but he was quickly demoted by the woman for his lack of respect for her orders, questioning under his breath, though not quietly enough or even with the intention of being unheard for that matter, how a female could command anyone or anything besides what he'd slip between her legs, and for his careless treatment and harsh hand with the animals that she often noticed. Having dropped by the stables from time to time, she had walked in on Wemple whacking the very same colt Samuel had tended to this morning and did not look kindly on the blood he had drawn from the filly's face and brow with his thin, sharp whip.

"How's it goin', Wemple." Samuel pulled the tall end of a nearby weed and snapped it and stuck the shorter end in his mouth.

"Expectin' somebody?" Wemple halted and stuck the handle end of his fork to the grass.

"Got my work done early, Wemp, thought I might break before startin' my evenin' chores. You need some help?"

Wemple started back towards the pile of shit that was

waiting for him, a detail he was to have tended to two days ago, one that Miss Stewart had given him hell for letting go. Samuel had witnessed the occasion and Miss Stewart's specific instruction for Wemple to do his own duties himself. "Naww, I got it, Flint. See yuh around."

Wemple was easy enough, Samuel thought, as he watched the twenty-something man scurry away, but, nonetheless, he decided to wait for Connie at the further end of the corral with the horses.

Connie heard a sharp whistle when she crossed past the shrubs. She paused briefly, looking for its source, and again, the sharp shrill beckoned her. She pinpointed from where it came and looked to the back of the corral. Samuel stood on one of the bottom boards and waved his arms above his head and pointed for her to travel along the far side of the corral, next to the line of trees.

He jumped down from where he stood and untied the horses' reins and led the two animals out the back gate. "Good afternoon, Connie McRamsee," he said, as he closed and latched the corral gate and the young lady approached.

"How do you do today, Samuel?"

He handed her the reins to her horse. "Couldn't be better." He pointed to his animal. "Decided to bring one of my own today."

"I see that, and he is lovely."

"She, Miss Connie—she is lovely."

"Oh, yes—well, of course." They laughed lightly and Connie looked at the bare back of her horse.

"Something wrong, Miss Connie?" Samuel saw her remotely lowered brows.

"No. Not at all."

"All right, then. Let's get to it." He helped Connie onto her horse and then hopped on his. The two headed down the bridle path they had followed the other day, but rather than stopping at the clearing, Samuel veered them off and they rode on a footpath along the edge of the pond for forty-five minutes or so, until they reached the water's far side, which blistered out into an attached smaller pond surrounded by trees and brush, but with a shore enough to sit along.

The blister pond was at least thirty feet in circumference and was one of the sources for its mother pond. The glorified pool was only seven or eight feet deep towards its center and, underneath it, bubbled an endless spring of clear, cold water. Samuel had discovered it during his first week at The Water's Edge Inn, and the footpath they had followed had only been traveled on by his boots until today.

When they had reached their destination, Samuel signaled Connie with a "Right here," and the two climbed off their horses and tied the reins to two trees, further from the pond's edge and in the shade. Samuel and Connie, on the contrary, moved towards the shore and the sun.

"How will this do?" Samuel found a grassier portion of the water's edge where they could sit.

Connie explored the cattails and reeds and the still, but slightly rippling surface of the pond. His question did not need a verbal reply. They seated themselves, and Connie laid down her parasol beside her and reached for her purse.

"Right down to business, I see, Miss McRamsee. I like that."

"Absolutely, Samuel. I'm not sure how long I can be away today, soo…" Her face heated with the bit of guilt that accompanied her words.

"Not a problem at all, Miss McRamsee. What will we be…imbibing today…the same one I saw you readin' I hope?"

Samuel took the small brown book that Cornelia held forward. "*Leaves of Grass* by Walt Whitman." He shrugged. "Never heard of him."

"He is an American poet, Samuel, and—and he celebrates nature and the soul and the body and his words—his words…" Connie's own words failed her. She took the book and opened it randomly to a page and handed it back to Samuel.

He scanned it. "All right, says this is from 'Song of Myself.'"

"Wonderful, one of his greatest. Go on."

"OK. Has a '5' above it." His eyebrows raised a second, and then he cleared his throat.

"I believe in you my soul, the other I am must not
abase itself to you,
And you must not be abased to the other.

Loafe with me on the grass, loose the stop from
your throat,
Not words, not music or rhyme I want, not
custom, or lecture, not even the best,
Only the lull I like, the hum of your valved voice."

He looked up. "I'm not sure what all that's about, Connie."

Walt Whitman's words had waved across Connie and as Samuel did his best to read the poetry, she looked towards the reflecting water and rising pine trees and then up at the clear soft blue sky…and back at Samuel. "Just continue, you're doing fine. You will see."

"All right, if you say so." Samuel flipped a couple pages. "Same poem, I guess, number '11.'

"Twenty-eight young men bathe by the shore,
Twenty-eight young men and all so friendly;
Twenty-eight years of womanly life and all so
lonesome.
She owns the fine house by the rise of the bank,
She hides handsome and richly drest aft the
blinds of the window.

Which of the young men does she like the best?
Ah the homeliest of them is beautiful to her.

Where are you off to, lady? for I see you,
You splash in the water there, yet stay stock still
in your room."

Samuel had accentuated some words, like "young" and "Ah," from this passage without try, and when he had finished he, again, looked up from his book and at Connie. He grinned broadly. "What do yuh got me readin' here, Miss McRamsee?"

"Do you like it, Samuel?"

"I reckon I do, Connie, though I ain't sure exactly where Mr. Whitman is going. I mean, I got an idea, but…"

"Shall I read some?" Connie reached for the open book and Samuel handed it to her.

The sun seemed to sit almost directly above the two.

She let her fingers work a few pages further from where Samuel had read, then began:

"You sea! I resign myself to you also—I guess what you mean,
I behold from the beach your crooked inviting fingers,
I believe you refuse to go back without feeling of me,
We must have a turn together, I undress, hurry me out of sight of the land,
Cushion me soft, rock me in billowy drowse,
Dash me with amorous wet, I can repay you."

She looked up at Samuel as he waited for her to continue. "Good, isn't it, Samuel. His words, they take you somewhere, I am sorry I fall short in explaining for you their significance and, at times, I am not really sure myself, but they take you somewhere, don't they?" She looked hastily back down at the book and then back at Samuel's face and his dark green eyes. "Don't you think?"

Samuel felt the sun's heat on the scalp beneath his sandy hair. He felt a trickle of sweat emerge from his hairline and frolic down his forehead and then break in his right brow.

He sat quiet a moment, without answering Connie……

"Ol' Walt takes me somewhere all right." He stood up in one quick movement on his long legs and began to unbutton his shirt. "We ain't got the sea here, Connie, but we do got one of the finest, freshest springs in the Adirondacks bubblin' up right next to us." He removed his shirt and bent to untie his boots.

"Samuel Flint, what on earth?"

He looked up at her from his task, his lightly streaked hair dangling in his eyes. His glance-up found Cornelia's eyes at nearly the same level, as she sat and watched him.

"Twenty-eight men swimmin' and dash me with your wet amorous sea! Hotter than hell sittin' here—pardon my language—and no other thing to do, Miss Cornelia McRamsee—let's take a swim!" He pulled off his unlaced boots and his socks, and dropped his pants, ran into the water in his long johns and dove beneath the surface.

Connie heard the horses a few feet off chewing on their grass. They had looked up at the scene by the water's edge.

A bee buzzed.

Seconds later Samuel spurted up from the center of the miniature pond. "WHEEEWWW! Come on, Connie, what are yuh waitin' for?" he yelled as if she were a mile off.

She set the book in the grass, stood up and cupped her hands around her mouth to shout. "Samuel, surely you can't expect me to just—to just undress here and jump in." She walked to the edge and bent, sticking her hand in the water. "Besides, it feels much too cold."

"Naw, it's fine until you get out here closer to the heart of the spring, but it feels damn good. Look at that sun." He squinted towards the globe of light and then re-submerged and attempted a handstand. When he resurfaced, he shook his wet head and palmed his hair off his eyes and face. "What's the matter?"

Connie stood where she had been bending, hands on hips. She raised her shoulders some and shook her head. "I just can't, Samuel. I can't."

"Aww, you're just like that lady, Connie. What's he say—she stays still in her room when she really wants to splash around." He started lapping his way to the further end of the pool, towards its shared side with the bigger one.

"Wait, Samuel Flint."

Samuel turned. Connie was sitting on the shore now, taking her boots off. "Help me out of this God forsaken dress, would you?"

He stroked the distance to where she stood and she had her boots off. They laughed and he walked from the water and helped her with her buttons and corset. "You're wet," she said, as he dripped water and formed a small puddle beneath him. The task was done more quickly than Connie had ever experienced before and she stood only for a second in her nainsook camisole and lace-trimmed knickers, and then jumped into the pond with Samuel close behind.

The surface was warm, but where her feet found the soft silt on the base, the water lay cooler. The two dove beneath the exterior and Samuel led her to where the spring flowed forth, he used his leg to direct Connie's, so her toes were above the gurgling current.

They popped their heads from the water for air.

"Feel?"

"What a strange sensation," she said with a simpering expression, as she immediately worked her left largest toe nearer the source.

Samuel dove beneath the surface again, the way a trout does after he leaps to swallow a fly.

Connie followed his underwater path with her eyes, guessing where he might surface. She flipped on her back, fanning her arms, and began to propel herself across the water. She fluttered along and let the sun reach her nose when she closed her eyes. Its arms warmed it within seconds and she wondered how something so far could reach out and find the tip of her face. Before any answers could possibly penetrate, a hundred droplets of splash hit her upper body and face.

As if she had been awakened from a winter's nap, she stood upright and tried to find the bottom of the pond. Before she could, another wave washed her.

A few feet away, Samuel stood in water to his shoulders, laughing and extending his arm to send another shower her way.

"Samuel!" She started towards him and the water from

his next bombardment flooded her. "You—you son of a—"

Samuel mocked shock, eyebrows raised and jaw dropped. "Uut, uut, watch your tongue, Miss Connie," he said, sending one more unretaliated spatter of huge droplets at her.

As she neared him, Connie spread both of her arms and then drew them across the pond's surface several times, pummeling Samuel with a clearly much better form of fire.

A war of water followed with shrieks and laughs and howls, and continued for several minutes.

"All right! All right!" Samuel shouted over sounds of pond rapidly leaving and returning to its whole. He began to retreat towards the shore, water still flying about him.

"Say uncle, Samuel, say uncle!"

"Never, Connie! Never!" Samuel broke into a run as soon as the water was knee-high, his revenger following closely behind.

He collapsed to the green grass where they had been sitting, where their clothes and the book they had been reading lay scattered about. Connie, a second later landed beside him, amongst their mess.

Breathing heavily from their brawl, they lay on their backs, their chests rising and falling rapidly.

Silence.

Only birds babbled with chirps, thick leaves of cattails rubbed one another in the almost nonexistent breeze.

Then a wild laughter erupted. It poured from Samuel and Connie, uncontrollable, unstoppable, with no sound reason.

They remained on their backs within a foot or less from each other with the sun already warming them, and they turned their heads to face one another, looking into each others mirthy eyes, continuing to laugh.

Between a mutual gasp for air, they heard Connie's appaloosa whinny. They rolled to their sides to look at the animal as it stood watching them lying there on the grass.

It hoofed the ground twice and shook its head back and forth, shooing a bug from its ears. And as it did, Connie and

Samuel's laughter didn't come to a thrashing halt, like a wailing sledge bouncing off a bar of steel, but instead, it faded and died out, each of the two almost taking a turn to keep it alive before it could no longer accompany the birds and cattails in their symphony or fill the woods as it had just done.

"Samuel." Connie was the first to speak. She sat up, propping herself with her hands extended behind her. She looked to the far distance of the larger pond. "It's been a wonderful afternoon, it has, but, as I said—" She turned to look at him.

Samuel remained horizontal and rested his head on fist, elbow in the grass. With his other hand he pulled a blade and placed it between his teeth. "You've got a prior engagement, Miss Connie. Yes, I know." He sat up. "Fill me with this crazy poetry and then you can't stay, huh? I see." He smiled and stood, extending his arms. "Let's get you back in Water's Edge Inn-ly order, shan't we."

Connie accepted his hands and, with his aid, stood. "You are too good to me, Samuel Flint. You do know that."

Hands still lightly clasped, they stood, noses and chests nearly touching.

"You're worth it," he said, tipping his head slightly.

The appaloosa neighed loudly once more, and they both stepped back.

And reaching for their clothes, they began to dress.

Chapter Eleven

Robert Stimes dragged on a cigarette and stared at the flourishing green shrubbery and the tops of the stables and barn roofs that jutted above and behind it. He had decided to take his lunch of broiled trout, doused in lemon and garlic sauce, on the back lawn where a few tables sat as an alternative to front lawn dining. Most or nearly all of the guests chose to dine on the opposite side from where Stimes sat today because of the degree of shade that the resort itself and some surrounding tress provided for them there.

Stimes had not removed his black top hat and coat, but rather, he sat in them and, just once, when he felt the sun warm his shoulders and bring forth perspiration from under his arms and in the groove of his crossed legs, did he say "The hell with you, damnedable ball of fire" under his breath. Servants came to refill his water glass, but each time they were greeted with Stimes's white-gloved hand covering its mouth. Instead, he would ting his crystal wineglass with his fork, and the servants would either pour what remained in the bottle of dry white that sat at the table or run and fetch him another one. They were not paid to question the peculiar habits of the rich guests and they knew this because the bottle of wine they carried often cost Pottash more than their entire summer's wages.

When Stimes had finished his plate and drank enough for two or three men, he lit the cigarette he pulled from his gold case. He smoked one and then another and he sat holding this third, sucking in its smoke and then twisting the fumes toward the sky. He had not decided what action to take, he did not stand for being lied to, this he knew. "Still, she is—she needs to be handled delicately," he said aloud. He looked to his left, then to his right. He was alone.

He took one more long breath of smoke so that he could feel it penetrate his gut, and then headed for the opening in the hedge…

For the good part of an hour, Wemple had been shoveling horse shit into a wheelbarrow, which he would then haul to the farthest end of the last barn and dump. Sweat streamed off his skinny body and he was leaning against the pitchfork when he heard the hard clumping of boots as someone strode in and onto the hardwood floor. He quickly wiped his forehead with a handkerchief and returned to the pile. Goddamn wench, he thought, checkin'

up on me again.

But over the stink of his own perspiration and the horse dung, he smelled...he thought for a second...yes, a fine cigarette, and a porter of wine the second time around. He turned and saw one of Pottash's male guests standing behind him. He brushed his work shirt with his sooted hand. "Good afternoon, sir, what can I do you for?" He attempted to smile, but his burning red face declined his brain's invitation. He, instead, extended his arm.

"I'm looking for a lovely young lady. Dark hair, today in a green dress, about so tall." Stimes, rather than shaking the foul young man's hand that was before him, raised his own to above his shoulders to designate this height of whom he sought. "You could not miss her beauty if you've seen her."

Wemple had played craps in the backstreets of Schenectady behind the ill-reputed Firestone Fanny's and had scooted rats away from the boards that would be his bed that night. He smelled a pile of shit, but it was not the one he had been forking into. "Can I get a cigarette from yuh?" he asked, leaning his fork on a stall wall and stepping a little closer to his visitor. The man handed him a smoke from his elegant case. He lit Wemple.

Goddamn fine tobacco. Wemple forced a smile then and his dirty yellow teeth held the cigarette that he would leave in his mouth until his conversation had ended. "I mighta seen this girl, Mr..." He waited for assistance.

"Either you have or you have not, boy. Now which is it?" Stimes had done his own share of shuffling the poker deck and dropping the marble.

"She your daughter?" Wemple called Stimes's bluff, the wine on the man's breath would shame his own mother.

Within two seconds, Wemple was bent, doubled over from the blast of fist to his stomach. His lips squeezed tightly around the cigarette, but managed to contain it. Smoke rolled up and stung his eyes. "Yeah, yeah, I seen her, not today though," he grumbled, trying to stand fully erect. "This pretty one, she don't ride in the morning with the other guests…"

The wine in Stimes's stomach curdled like milk in the summer sun as it mixed with his natural liquids. He bent toward Wemple. "Continue…"

"Yeah, she came around late, one other time." Wemple would enjoy his next words. He stood fully again and his gut ached, but he inhaled his drag and let it stream slowly into Stimes's face. "She came back ridin' the other day, sharin' the same horse with a guy who works here…and she was lookin' like she liked it, Mister, a lot." A wheezy, grunted laugh followed and Stimes's fist put an end to it.

Wemple's cigarette fell from his mouth and he again hunched. Lifting his foot with the little strength he could muster, he stepped the butt out with the shit-soiled sole of his boot and looked up without moving his head.

The man before him was reaching into pocket, he pulled out a silver clip with a wad. Wemple watched as he separated three bills from it and tossed them on the stable floor. "You will keep me posted, lad. Good day."

When the sound of boots to the floor ceased, Wemple, still wheezing, dropped to his knees and grabbed the money. Three twenties felt like his hard dick in his hand, he began to laugh, kissing and caressing them. He stuffed his easy earn in his pocket and then savagely sifted through the loose chaff on the floor. The smoke he had dropped had at least three good drags left to it.

Cornelia closed the suite's door behind her. She heard the grandfather clock's tick…tick…tick. As she passed the open way of the parlor on her route to her room, she heard the lips of her father, the pup, pup sound they made as he sucked to get the cigar that he held lit. She turned to see the back of his head and the glow of his light in front of him. "Cornelia," he said without turning, "we need to speak."

She walked into the parlor with its brick and brass fireplace obsolete in July and china cabinets filled with dishware eaten on by royalty that they would never touch. She seated herself on the opposite couch, where Mr. McRamsee and Robert Stimes had seated themselves that same morning. She propped her parasol on the end table, placed her purse beside her, pressed her dress down her lap with her gloved hands. "Yes, Father."

Henry McRamsee had been born into money, not to say, he did not do his best to add to the family fortune because, by all means, he had. He continued to buy textile and leather mills north of Albany in Amsterdam and Gloversville and Johnstown. He was wealthy. He traveled six months of the year, part business, always searching for better production methods, part pleasure, always seeking women, never completely robbing them of their chastity, but, instead, just buying them dinner and a diamond here and there. He had wanted his wife to birth him a son, to carry the name and the business and all that glorious bullshit that men like Henry McRamsee worry about, but she had not, and after Cornelia, could not. So, he sat facing his only heir.

He doused his light with the lid and set it on the table, and tasted his cigar. "Connie, dear, what are you doing to your mother and me?"

Connie knew to wait.

The end of his cigar glowed again as he inhaled. "Where do you find such nonsense? Did that whore on Temple Street sell it to you? Nothing but a lunatic whore she is, Connie. You are immediately to hand over that rubbish which you entertained all with while dining yesterday."

Connie looked at her graying father in his evening suit, black and white attire and bow tie. His tall hat sitting beside him, brandy in front of him. She was finished with the book, anyway. Her friend, Annie, a middle-aged, used bookstore owner, perhaps down on her luck but never a whore, would order her another copy when she returned to Albany in the fall. She reached for and in her purse, and pulled out the small brown book. "Certainly, Father. I am truly sor—"

Henry McRamsee leaned forward and swiped his hand across the coffee table between them, sending his goblet of brandy flying and then smashing into the fireplace to their right. "Do *not* pull that apologetic bullshit with your father, Cornelia. Your mother may buy it, Mr. Stimes may engage in it, but I am the last person who will put up with it. My mother was a loose cannon, Connie, and I see her in you, daughter, I see that wild fire in your damnedable eyes the way I saw it in hers when I was a little boy and, even more so, as I grew and tried to help my father with the business." He held his cigar and slammed his fist. "Do you understand me? This small empire I have built will continue to grow, Connie. You will read what we say and do as we say and marry who we say, mixing ours with good blood, producing grandchildren galore. Perhaps, even a young Henry to look after it all, aye?" His words lightened, as the image of his grandson walking the factory floor with him filled his brain. "Connie. We know what is best. Is this understood...do you understand?"

Connie sat, her bag on her lap, her hands folded and holding the book. She leaned forward and handed Walt Whitman across the table. "Yes, Father, I understand."

Mr. McRamsee took the book and held it from his fading eyes. "*Leaves of Grass*, very well then. If you insist on reading, Connie, perhaps a book from Pottash's selection from the downstairs library. A classic? Maybe a good Shakespearean play, a history play, the Henry plays might be suitable, aah, yes, quite suitable for you, or if you insist, perhaps, another."

"I hear he is a fine playwright, Father. Yes, a Shakespeare will do."

The clock donged for the five o'clock hour.

"Very well, then. Your mother waits for us in the main dining room. I shall tell her you won't be long—and that all is well that ends well?"

Connie nodded. Henry McRamsee rose and she followed his lead. "I will be just a short time freshening up, Father."

She excused herself and left the parlor, Henry would finish his cigar and *then* he could see to his waiting wife. He ran his finger across the page edges of the book he still held. "Puuh—*Leaves of Grass*." He walked to the fireplace, crunching across the broken brandy glass and splattering even further the small puddles of sweet liquid. The servant would attend to it. He pressed the lit end of his cigar against the bottom corner of the pages and threw the smoking book behind the dark screen and into the pile of cedar logs that lay there.

Connie bathed that night after dinner, more for removing the scent of the several ounces of perfume she had doused herself with a few hours earlier in an effort to conceal any smell of outdoor or animal that may have lingered from her session with Samuel. Earlier, she had stood turned 'round and viewed herself in her full-length, attempting to detect any stains on the bottom of her dress, as those that Miss Stewart had noticed the day before. Perhaps, because the dress was darker it had not been dirtied, so, Connie simply sprayed herself with her L'eau des Riches and proceeded hurriedly to dinner.

Upon drying herself and powdering her body, she wanted nothing but sleep. However, under her fresh, cool sheets, she lay alone, without its company and cradling. Once or twice it did seal shut her eyes, but only momentarily, for the muggy night air made breathing a work, and her body ached, from what she did not know. Perhaps her ride...her swim...something else? She heard the clock outside her door strike midnight, and she rose and robed herself.

The suite glowed quietly with the moonlight from the picture window in its parlor. Tall shadows and silhouettes stretched across furniture and floor, and, from her open doorframe, Connie studied the life-size watercolor of blues and blacks. Though her mission would be innocent enough,

Connie instinctively looked towards the room beside the study, her parents' room. Their door closed, Connie knew they shared these quarters, but not a bed.

Dim lights were left on in the hallways of The Water's Edge Inn. Some gentlemen lingered late at the bar lounge, mothers walked young children who could not sleep. Pottash saw to all needs of every guest. Tonight, he lit the way for Cornelia McRamsee as she made her way, barefoot, down the great staircase and to the resort library for a copy of Shakespeare.

She could hear nothing but her footsteps on the stairs, the day's heat having extinguished all the other guests' short city fuses. She descended and crossed right, down the hall that lay opposite the breakfast room. This hall housed the more business end of the inn—the library, a few offices for those who could not leave work behind, perhaps one or two significant servants' quarters, and even a lecture hall for guest orators or visiting politicians, yet to be used. Even during the day, this end seemed to echo only the opening or closing of a door or the hurried gait of an ambitious man's walk.

Connie walked to the far end of the huge hall and stood before the last door on the right, a twelve foot high mound of oak, one with a gold-plated sign engraved with the words "The Water's Edge Inn Library: QUIET." She turned the knob, and it being unlocked, she entered.

The crystal chandelier hanging from the center of the ceiling must be left on at all times, Connie thought, but as her eyes focused to the room's lighting, she realized that it was not lit at all and that it hung from a spectacular dome of glass, which the moon's light immigrated through.

Connie moved forward, slowly, looking up at times. The white radiance filled the room, lighting the space, letting alone the high wooden shelves and scattered desks and tables, these remaining dark. Some books' bindings caught the translucent glow, but these were few and only those that contained elusive lettering.

When Connie stood just below the chandelier, she halted, placing her hands on the top of a desk and tipping her head further upward. She wanted then only to bathe in this light, it poured over her now, like a weightless waterfall, but she wanted more of it…she turned her head down and towards the door. She had closed it. In a single motion she untied the belt of her satin robe and let it drop to the floor. Her arms exposed and the base of her neck, she looked again, beyond the light fixture and the domed glass. The moon, roving with quite less than a full face tonight, stared back. It, too, seemingly enjoyed her company, and with this thought, she laughed smally. She outstretched her arms toward the shower and its source. She had tried to distract her base intention in doing so, and stood as such just for a moment, until her hands lowered and pulled the neck string of her thin white cotton nightgown. She widened the hole and let the garment slip from her body, until it lay around her feet. Here, she stood, back arched, hands pressed on the desk before her, facing upward.

As the eye above sent the sun's light towards her in its own sequestered and unabashed fashion, Connie's skin glowed palely with and in it. She stood, statuesque, until her knees weakened and she bent down, hands still atop the desk. She rested her head between them and she began to cry. To cry quietly as the streams of tears poured forth from her eyes. She felt some of the warm droplets streak down and roll off her chin and journey as far as her bare thighs. She wiped some with the back of her hands and then with her fingertips, and, still, she tasted the salt of others as her mouth curved tightly downward, opening for the breaths of air and the exits of small sounds of a deep sadness.

Connie had not heard the creak, nor seen the long crack of the oak door as it was pushed slightly open. Only until the dim, different light of the hallway intruded on her world, as it turned from a thin, lengthy strip to an inch or more of straight, did Connie turn her head towards it. "Is there someone in there?" she heard a quieted, familiar voice ask.

"One moment, please," Connie answered, wiping tears and pulling the nightgown back over body and slipping into its arms. She pulled and tied her neck string, just as the voice asked "Miss?" and its mistress, hearing no reply, slowly opened the door and entered.

For the second time that day Miss Eliza Stewart's and the young Connie McRamsee's eyes met. The servant broke the gaze only to close the door behind her. "Dear me, what are yuh doin' up so late and in here, Miss McRamsee? Yuh look like yuh've seen a ghost." The head servant, in her housecoat, came towards Connie and picked the robe off from the floor and placed it around the girl's shoulders. "Are yuh all right, Miss Cornelia?"

"Good evening, Miss Stewart," Connie managed, accepting the robe. Eliza took her hand and led her to a table with a few chairs around it. She sat her down and then pulled one up close to her and seated herself.

Connie looked down at her ten thin fingers folded neatly in her lap.

"Miss McRamsee," Eliza hesitated in word and in action as she placed her hands on those of Connie. "You got troubles, I know this, girl, and I see what you're up to. I'm not sure if it is all good and I ain't sure if it is all that bad either, but what I am sure'a is that you're a beautiful young girl with a whole lotta spark, spark that could get yuh into a fix, but spark that could get yuh outa a fix too. And what I am about to say, others—" she nodded her head towards the door as if those she spoke of stood outside of it, "others would call it damn lousy advice, but I say different.

"Some, they're made of water. Sure, they might start out as a lake or even a waterfall, but sure as hell they turn into a pond or puddle and dry up sooner or later. They spend half their lives sayin' 'I shoulda' or 'I wish.' But, you, you're all fire, I don't have to know you that well to see that. And that boy, Samuel Flint—"

Connie looked up then, blushing lightly across her cheekbones.

"Aye, he's got a fire too, Connie, like you. A lot of those pools of piss will try to spray the both of yuhs out, but..." Miss Stewart stopped and took her hand from Connie's pair and placed it under the girl's chin, their eyes held encounter now, and, with this short accomplishment, Eliza repositioned her fingers across the soft brims of young womanly knuckles and tucked her tips in the quiet, curved palms. "Don't let 'em do it to yuh, girl. Neither of yuh will be spendin' your words with 'I shoulda's' or 'I wish I'da.' You're the ones who'll be sayin' 'I did' and 'I will.' Do yuh see, Miss McRamsee? You won't end up wipin' the arses of rich folks like I have, but it might be something worse if yuh don't put your head to the bare earth and listen to what's leadin' yuh forward. Now...let's wipe what's left under your eyes." Miss Stewart swiped her thumb under each of Connie's eyes and stood then—and threw the costume of top servant back over her head, or so it seemed to Connie. "Are yuh needin' a book to get yuh back to sleep, Miss Connie?" She cupped her hands in front of her bosom and looked up at and across the stacks.

"I'm looking for something by Shakespeare, Miss Stewart. A Henry play, perhaps." Connie stood to follow the already moving woman.

"He's over here, Miss Cornelia, at an arm's length. Won't be needin' to climb one of those long ladders for W. Shakespeare." Eliza studied the shelves she came to, scanning the S's. She tsked her tongue and ran her pointer finger across the bindings until she landed on the Shakespeares. "Here we are—Henrys, yuh say?" She followed past tragedies and comedies and histories and ran by collections of sonnets. "Let's see, we got Richard—" She scooted her hand back to Shakespeare's H's. "Right next to him is young Hen. Will...this one do?" she asked as she pulled it from the shelf and handed it to Connie, who immediately examined the gray cover with maroon lettering.

"It is on my father's recommendation, of course." Connie said, looking at Miss Stewart.

The woman only raised her right brow slightly. "Of course."

"But Miss Stewart, I will grab another while I am here. Could you perhaps suggest one?"

Eliza's cheeks rounded. "Aah, Miss McRamsee, I am no Shakespearean scholar, but seein' that your father picked that one, I might suggest one towards the opposite end of the shelf." She turned and randomly removed a smaller red bound book, one that was ten or twelve down from the one she had previously pulled, and handed it to Connie. She winked then. "Have a good night, Miss."

Connie turned the book over in her hand and placed it on top of her new borrowed copy of *Henry the Fourth: Part One*. The silver-lettered title read *Romeo and Juliet*.

………"I took Shakespeare to bed that night, but didn't read him. I knew that I would carry *Henry* around The Water's Edge, read it for show, perhaps act so taken with the book that I could avoid conversing until I could clearly decide what path I would take, although I knew I had already chosen."

"Gram, I don't understand, I mean, none of this, you never…"

"No, Matthew, I never have told anyone. But today, I can't say why—not for sure anyway, but I think I am—something tells me that I am suppose to tell you."………

Chapter Twelve

When Samuel brought his first crate of bottled milk to The Water's Edge Inn kitchen the next morning he did as he had done the last few days, placing it down, grabbing a hard roll or croissant from one of the trays that sat on the counter, and eating it as one of the other servants brought the crate to the opposite end of the kitchen and dumped the bottles' contents in a pot for common kitchen use—filling creamers, baking tarts, pouring over fresh peaches, the list too lengthy.

Today, he leaned against the counter and chewed the final bite of a flaky cinnamon croissant and watched Raymond Grankster, a sixteen-year-old dining servant with a caterpillar moustache, bring the crate back through the kitchen crowd. Samuel straightened himself, ready to take his goods back for a second fill and expecting no real verbal exchange with the boy, as Grankster took his profession very seriously and saw any unnecessary conversation as a distraction from his purpose there.

This morning, however, in the passing, Grankster, choosing as few words as possible so he could return to his pancake batter much faster, said, "Miss Stewart wants a check of your bottles next run." He turned and the words "Wait until someone fetches her when you come back" nearly lost themselves in the whips of beaters and sizzling of griddles and yells for orders before they reached Samuel's ears.

Samuel stood holding his crate for a moment in front of him. Wondering. Then he slapped it on his shoulder and opened the screen door, feeling sure enough that he would soon find out.

Forty-five minutes later, Samuel returned with his second delivery and he did not even bend to place it on the floor, but a passing servant, in such desperate need for the thick liquid, grabbed the crate from his hands and scurried it to the back. Samuel watched as the boy took one bottle and poured its fluid in the silver drum and then ladled some into a bowl of assorted fruit and dashed out of the kitchen with it.

The crate did not sit lonely, however, for the Raymond Grankster's recipe for crepe suzettes called for several cups of cream and he strode over to finish the dispensing. Samuel watched as each bottle exchanged milk for air with a glup...glup...glup flow.

In a matter of minutes, Grankster chalked another kitchen conquest on his imagination's blackboard, but, before returning Samuel's apparatus, he stuck his head into the kitchen office where Samuel saw the side of Miss Stewart sitting at her desk, as she, perhaps, looked over a payroll or menu plan. Samuel saw the woman look up from her work, then down the kitchen towards him and then answer words back to Grankster.

Ten seconds later, Raymond had woven his way through the kitchen once more and stood in front of Samuel. The caterpillar above the servant's lips wavily danced, though barely and briefly, as the words "Wait here" slipped off the rarely used tongue. The dozen or so empty bottles clanked and rattled some, as he set the crate down in front of Samuel.

And no sooner had Samuel looked down and then up again, Miss Stewart had made her way from the office to the door at which he stood. Her face firm and reddened from a morning of waking with the rooster and cooking for a lot of two-hundred and managing a sometimes less than ambitious staff, she succeeded in passing a pleasant "Good morning" to Samuel as she came closer to him.

"Good morning, Miss Stewart, you'll be needin' to look at my sparklin' clean milk bottles, I hear."

The look on Miss Eliza Stewart's face indicated nothing of the like for a second and Samuel noticed that she seemed to have to remind herself of her set purpose. "Aah, yes, Samuel, are you doin' right by these trusty things?" She squatted and pulled a few of the bottles halfway from the crate and looked into them. Samuel pulled his trousers some and bent at the knees, as well.

"Miss Stewart?"

Servants passed to and fro, in and out of the breakfast room and the door to the back lawn where they were also serving and setting tables. Some glanced at the seemingly routine checkup, while others ignored the two completely.

Miss Stewart looked up, at an exact moment when the traffic seemed to have ceased. "Aye, this one may have a crack," she said, and as she tipped it towards her, she reached in the front pocket of her apron and pulled out a folded piece of paper and stuffed it in the mouth of the empty milk-coated bottle. As quickly as the bottle clanged back in place, Eliza stood. "Yuh may want to check that one, Samuel, maybe replace it, if need be."

And Samuel, still squatting, looked up at her.

"Don't be waitin' all day, Flint, you got one more run, don't yuh?" She gave a wave, as if shooing a cat off from a counter.

He stood with his crate and nodded as one does when he uses his head for a handshake. "That I do, Miss Stewart."

Both turned and then returned to their duties as Pottash servants.

When Samuel entered the barn, his remaining Guernsey turned her brown eyes toward him as she invited him to narrow her bulging bag.

"One second, girl, got some business here first." He set the crate on the small counter which he used for his daily milk pouring deed.

Sticking his fingers into the mouth of the center bottle that Miss Stewart had put the paper in, he stretched his hand down. He stretched it again and turned it some, but the paper sat too low in its container. He removed his fingers from the bottle and then the bottle from the crate. As he tipped the thick glass upside down, a few droplets of foamy cream formed at its mouth and dropped on his boot, but, with this, the letter had also slipped towards the opening and Samuel once more reached his pointer and middle finger past the bottle's lip. This time, with little maneuvering, Samuel seated the curved, folded sheet between the cleft of his two fingers and pulled it forth.

He looked around, although already knowing he had the barn to himself, all the other hands avoiding his three ladies, as no one had the patience or energy to deal with their kicking hooves or large teats except for him. He stood closer, letter in hand, to the open back window that allowed the morning sun to light the stalls and his workbench.

The paper he held seemed old, with a ripped edge, as if...he thought, maybe torn from a book. He opened it, and though it had soaked drops of cream here and there, it was far from illegible.

Dear Samuel,

I am sorry that I must cancel our plans to ride today and read. I am forced to spend the day here on the grounds for reasons you may have guessed and that I will be more than willing to explain in detail later. However, as there is a program of music set for the concert hall tonight, a seated gala of sorts, I do think I will be able to slip away. I am running out of room on this dreadful page, so I will meet you at 8 o'clock behind the corral.

Please be there, I look forward, Connie.

Samuel looked up. He squinted as the sun's rays crossed the treetops and stretched to the window frame at which he stood. He returned his eyes to the letter, and with the bobbing ball of white light that forms in one's sight after looking too directly at the sun, he noticed a small arrow on the bottom of the page. Following its direction, he flipped the sheet over.

p.s. I hope you like Shakespeare—Tonight, C.M.M.

He folded the letter and buried it in his pocket and turned to the Guernsey. She stood, still staring, chewing her cud.

"Don't you tell nobody, girl, yuh hear, or you'll be beef before you know it," he said, grabbing his stool and pail from the wall and walking towards the animal.

She watched, as he stroked her side and seated himself beside her. "Naw, I'm just kiddin' with yuh, girl. You don't got any opinion on Shakespeare do yuh?" He looked at the cow's dark nose and her long dark eyelashes.

She blinked sleepily and turned her head towards the window.

"Didn't think so."

Squirts of milk ting'd and echoed off the bottom of the empty bucket as he began to pull on the cow's teats……

"What happened to Walt?"

The sun still sat high above the mountains as Connie approached Samuel that evening no more than a minute or two late for their rendezvous.

"You got the note?" Connie's eyes smiled.

"Yes, Miss Stewart passed it along. She's a peach, that one." Samuel untied the horses' reins and handed a set over to Connie. Her rich dark blue dress with black buttons down its front hugged her figure and she had braided her ebony hair loosely and let it lap over her right shoulder. "You look lovely tonight, Miss McRamsee, if you don't mind me sayin'."

She took the reins of the appaloosa from Samuel and scratched the animal's chin. "Hello, girl," she addressed the horse, which had begun to take a liking to its most frequent rider, and then she looked back to Samuel, who, she had immediately observed, had cleanly shaven himself and brought his hair back from his forehead quite handsomely and, in doing so, showed off his dark green eyes. "Likewise, Mr. Flint."

Samuel smiled as he looked to the grass beneath his feet. She *had* noticed.

"As for Walt, he met an untimely demise, Samuel. A story not worth repeating. But we now have William." Samuel helped her onto her horse and Connie continued, "And as for Miss Stewart," she breathed in and looked towards the mountains, "she is much more than that, Samuel. I could not use writing paper as my parents would inquire to whom I was writing, so I ripped a blank page out of the back of this book." She patted her purse. "And I passed it along to her when I arrived early in the breakfast room this morning."

Samuel had listened as he mounted his horse. "What's the matter, Connie? The ol' man might not take you readin' poetry with the stable guy so good?"

"Samuel, it's not that, well, you see—"

Samuel began to move his horse towards the far left of the backend of the corral. "Connie, I'm just givin' yuh a little grease, we do that up here in these parts. Now, I can guess you ain't got that much time out here tonight, and I think you're ready for a slow run with that girl, that is if you're up to it."

They rode, walking their horses at a slow pace, in the small space parallel and between the spread of trees on their right and the fence line on their left.

"I am, you can be sure of that," she voiced to the tall, almost lanky, but broad-shouldered young man in front of her.

"All right then, let's get goin'." And with that, Samuel gave his horse a kick and they took off with a quick canter.

Connie probed her horse with her feet as she had seen Samuel do, but the horse merely acknowledged her action with a jerk of its body and then simply resumed walking. "Samuel, wait. She—refuses to cooperate."

Samuel was already some distance ahead of her now and was turning up a narrow path into the woods. "Don't be afraid of her, Connie. Give her a jab." He disappeared into the trees.

"Jab," Connie said aloud to herself and gave a weak whack with her feet again. No reaction. She tightened her hands on the reins. "Hyaa!" she announced and shot the back of her boots into the appaloosa's ribs, and, with that, the two began to lope at a strong pace.

......Samuel led them along, not slowing his pace once, as he had heard the easy trot of Connie's horse come up behind him shortly after he entered the trees. The pair gaited along for more than a half-hour on the barely path which exercised its mountainous liberty to hill itself when it saw fit and round and wrap itself through clumps of trees, not twisting like a crooked climbing rose, but wandering more like a drunken man destined for home on a Sunday morning. And in places, branches hung rather low, and at times, the riders needed to bend forward and cling to their horses to avoid being thrown. Still, Samuel, with no abatement in action, moved them forward.

He did turn, just once and without Connie's notice, as his horse jumped a small gully that crossed their way. His faith that Connie could handle her horse seemed without end, but, even so, a different instinct or intuition overtook him and he watched, as she bent low and enjoyed the leap her horse made.

A moment later, having almost cornered the path, Connie saw that they followed along side the very same gully they had just crossed. They followed it down a lengthy, slow rolling hill, and Connie watched as Samuel pulled his horse to a stop and sat atop waiting for her to do the same when she reached him.

Connie pulled back her reins as she trotted towards the bottom of the hill and then completely halted her horse beside Samuel's.

"You took to that horse, I'd say, like the way I took to your poetry, Connie. Truth is, probably even better."

"Have I broken her in, Samuel?"

"Aaah, not quite yet, but I'd say you're ready to, and besides, when you break that one in, you won't be askin' me. You'll know all right."

They breathed heavily, as if they had done the running themselves and as all do after riding a quick route tucked on the back of such regal animals.

Behind the two and their horses, a lazy creek, perhaps fifteen feet in width and only three or four feet at its deepest, accepted the long vein of water that had led the pair down the hill and to its mother.

Connie had been watching its waters wash over smooth rocks of all sizes, some just beneath the surface and others protruding just above it, when she felt Samuel beside her. He had dismounted without her notice and, smiling, he stood with an extended hand to help her down. She slid off her horse and they tied their animals to trees beside the smaller stream where it met flat ground and widened over a bed of moss and grass and pebbles, and creating a sort of mini-delta before losing itself into the wider waters.

"Feel like wadin'?" Samuel asked as he moved a tree's branch for Connie to come through and stand beside him on a surface of a million rounded stones at the water's edge.

Connie leaned forward slightly and with the lifted branch above her and trees to her either side, she almost felt as if a natural doorframe had been formed and Samuel was inviting her to enter another room. "I'm sorry?" she asked, now standing next to him.

Samuel looked the length of the creek as far as his eyes allowed or no obstruction of tree blocked or bend of the natural mirror's direction dissuaded him. For nearly a quarter of a mile, his eyes could follow the clear water with its whitecaps and waves and ripples, all so small and unassertive, charming more than seductive, but glittering under the evening sun. He retraced his eyes' route and landed back on a grand rock, more than six feet across and sitting with a slant, in the center of the creek not very far from where they stood.

"I said do you feel like wadin'?" He pointed towards the rock. "The way that sun is shinin' down out there, I'm thinkin' we'd have quite a study, with all that natural light and all." He squinted one eye and framed his hands then, the way an artist does as he tries to determine exactly what will end up on his canvas. He grinned and added, "Besides, it'd be fun."

Connie looked at the rock with its warm surface and slow moving skirt. She smiled. "I believe you have a very good point, Samuel."

They sat then, their feet extended towards one another. And as both began to unlace their own boots, their eyes strayed to the other's footwear, Samuel's with its hole in its left and its long rawhide leather laces and its shades of brown, lighter where the cuffs of his pants hung over and, where exposed, darker and soiled from the rough and work and weather, Connie's with its black strings and consistent, polished black surfaces, dignified by thin curves and slight heels and delicately swirled designs on its pointed toes, and scuffed only politely on its virgin soles that seemed suited best for marble floors.

And sometimes, an unobtrusive glance sent one's way sits like a feather on his—or her—shoulder, but however light it may be, it still does not go unnoticed by its receiver. So it was for both Samuel and Connie, as both briefly encountered the other's boots with their eyes.

Samuel spoke first. He pulled off his left boot and stuck his pinky finger in its rugged growing hole. "Just lets the air in a little, that's all. Reckon I might have to pick up a new pair sooner or later. But boots are funny things, ain't they? Some people mind 'em, some people don't."

Connie removed her right boot and was unclipping and pulling off a black stocking. "My friend Annie, the one who gave me the Whitman book, she says you can tell a lot about a person by the shoes they wear." She pulled the stocking off, and her bare foot touched the smooth stones.

Samuel had just about completed his business and was stuffing his socks in his boots. "I don't know about that one. If she's right, then, well, I think we're both in a lotta trouble. Don't you?" He stood and began to roll his pant legs to just below his knees.

Connie pulled at her left boot and set it beside her right

and then pulled down her other silk stocking. She paused. "Annie is usually right, Samuel, but, you have to see things the way she does." She tossed her stocking beside its mate and her boots, looped her purse around her wrist, and stood. "She will say to me if you can't find an answer to your question, you are asking the wrong question, or at the very least, asking it in the wrong way. You see?" She extended her arms from her sides as she took a few steps and her feet met the new surface.

"I think I like Annie already. Sounds like a friend of mine I'm hopin' you can meet. Maybe I'll meet her if I ever get down your way." Samuel, too, began to move towards the creek.

They stood at the water's edge for a moment, perhaps determining the best route. Connie spoke. "Yes. You would like her, Samuel. And she would like you very much." Samuel smiled and she reached her arm out then. "Now, sir, give me your hand—I don't want you slipping."

"Ahh, I see. You're too thoughtful," Samuel said, joining hands with Connie. As she lifted her dress's bottom to her knees, they moved into the summer cool water of Canterbury Creek.

It accepted them as if they were one of her own stones, washing quietly around their feet, creeping up their legs only as they stepped in a ditch formed by two medium-sized rocks.

"Where is down your way, anyway?" Samuel asked, looking over at Connie, who was deeply engrossed in the creek's bed and determining where to step next.

"I live in Albany, the heart of it. We are there only part of the year." Her foot glided on a slippery stone and the water's surface laughed approvingly. Connie's tipping body signaled the dropping of her dress's bottom from her left hand and the immediate grabbing of Samuel's shoulder.

And this sudden weight on the young man's left side shifted him so that he nearly lost his footing, as well. They stood for a second, Connie with the water lapping up around the lower fabrics of her dress and Samuel replanting his feet on the one bigger stone he had been aiming for when interrupted.

Looking at each other, the two's words burst and crossed.

"What are you doing?" and "That was you!" and "Well, I didn't intend on taking a swim tonight!" and "Well, I'm wet now!" and "It's not my fault!" intermingled, interrupted, and ended abruptly.

"The hell with it then!" Samuel, with a single motion, swept his arms behind and beneath Connie's back, and picked her up.

Connie's arms reflexed above his shoulders and around his neck and held tightly. "Samuel Flint, please, don't drop me!"

Samuel did not reply as he took a long step towards their destination. He stopped, as he decided where to place his bare feet, and then started forward again. He continued in this fashion, with Connie cradled like an overgrown infant in his arms, and making steps of a giant intervened with moments of a wizard's keen calculation, until he reached the huge rock.

He placed his right foot on its base beneath the water's surface. His bent leg formed a seat, allowing Connie to step down and instantly shape her feet with the higher, and dry, polished rock surface. She stood and turned, giving her hand to Samuel, and he accepted and stepped on with her. They stood looking at each other, Samuel's pants wet to his thighs and Connie's dress sopped around her legs.

Another shared laughter, this time accompanied by the lull of the water and the rata-tat-tat of a fiercely busy woodpecker in the distance and by the quietude of the Adirondack air, a sound in itself.

Words between hysterics and pointed fingers.

"You're soaked." Connie started.

"Thanks to you." Samuel finished.

They walked around this small island, as it brought back their attention. They stepped to its far edges, as if mapping it out. Big enough for the two of them, shaped like a tilting lounge. Nature's perfection.

"Good call, Samuel, nonetheless."

"Agreed upon then? Worth the trip?"

"Quite."

"So what'd you bring?" Samuel seated himself, Indian style on the higher end of the mass.

Connie had almost forgotten the purpose of their mission. "Oh, yes," she said, seating herself in much the same fashion and facing Samuel. "We have a play, actually." Connie pulled out the little red book and ran her hand across its cover. "We have one copy of a semi-wet *Romeo and Juliet* by William Shakespeare."

"This I've heard of," Samuel said, taking the book that Connie extended to him. He flipped through the pages. "The woman who used to live down the way from us, Louisa Bettan, an ol' gal but a smart one, had a buncha books, think she taught somewhere before she came home to take care of her dad. Anyway, she watched me before I was too young to help out on my folks' farm, she's mostly how I learned to read, yuh see." He stopped himself and looked up at Connie. She listened. "I know she had this book, I just never got to it. 'Bout two star-struck lovers, right?"

"Yes, I think they were star-struck or star-crossed perhaps, but that is the story. I have not read it yet myself. I thought we might read it as a play should be read."

"Actin' it out?"

"Well, not necessarily acting it, but each of us taking a part and then reading it." She set her hands on the rock and shifted her seat, such that she now sat next to Samuel. She suddenly felt the need to explain this action. "We won't have to pass the book this way. You can be Romeo and I'll read Juliet."

"Sounds good to me." Samuel closed the crack Connie had left between them, and opened the book. He flipped past the title page and Shakespeare bio and notes about the Globe, and came upon the first scene. "There's a whole lotta other names here..." He flipped a few more pages and stumbled across a Romeo. "And here, Romeo is talkin' to a Benvolio. I think—bein' pressed for time—don't you think we should get straight to our conversation?"

Connie nodded. "We may miss something important, but I think you are right, Samuel. Find where the two first speak."

Samuel turned a few more pages and then a few more. "Got Juliet now, but she's talkin' with a Nurse and Wife." He continued to pass through the act. "Here we go—we got Romeo and Juliet." He held the book between Connie and him, on their formed lap. "OK, says Romeo. 'If I profane with my unworthiest hand/This holy shrine, the gentle sin is this'... What?" He looked towards Connie and then back to the book. "OK, where am I? Yeah, here. 'My lips, two blushing pilgrims, ready stand/To smooth that rough touch with a tender kiss.' Uht-oh, she's in trouble. Here, it's you." He moved the book a little closer to Connie.

She moved her finger beneath the word Juliet and began. "'Good pilgrim, you do wrong your hand too much,/Which mannerly devotion shows in this;/For saints have hands that pilgrims' hands do touch,/And palm to palm is holy palmers kiss.'" She moved the book back towards Samuel.

He looked at Connie's face. "That was great," he said, and then followed her finger to Romeo. "'Have not saints lips, and holy palmers too?'"

Both held the book now and Connie raised it closer to her face. "'Ay, pilgrim, lips that they must use in prayer.'"

"'O, then, dear saint, let lips do what hands do!/They pray; grant thou, lest faith turn to despair.'"

"'Saints do not move, though grant for prayers' sake.'"

"'Then move not while my prayer's effect I take./Thus from my lips, by thine my sin is purged.'"

Connie had followed the Romeo line, not from the print as she had with his previous ones, but as she watched it recited from Samuel's curved lips. She saw Samuel smile after pronouncing his last word. "What?" she asked, "Why are you smiling?" Her eyes turned to the book to try to find her next line. "Now I've lost my place, I'm sorry."

Samuel said nothing, but instead moved his finger. Connie followed it as it passed "purged" and then moved across the stage direction "kisses her" and then stopped at Juliet. Her face grew warm. "Oh. Here we are," she said without looking up. "'Then have my lips the sin that they have took.'"

"'Sin from my lips? O trespass sweetly urged!/Give me my sin again.'"

They sat quiet a moment as they listened to the water circle their stage. "There it is again, Connie. Romeo's just an ol' dog, ain't he."

Connie gave a little laugh and ran her free hand down her braid.

"You're up, Juliet."

"'You kiss by th'book.'" She kept her hand on the braid and twined the end with her finger.

Samuel looked up from the book. "And we get the Nurse again." He looked back down and began flipping pages forward. "Whatta yuh say you read some Juliet for a while, you make it sound real well." He stopped on a lengthy Juliet speech and pecked it with his finger. "This one looks good."

Connie took the book now and held it across his and her leg. She turned slightly, as if reading to him. "'Though knowest the mask of night is on my face;/Else would a maiden blush bepaint my cheek/For that which thou hast heard me speak to-night.' Kiss me, now. I want you to kiss me."

Samuel watched her read the lines, her full pinkish lips trying their hardest to accentuate the sounds and syllables. He watched her green eyes as they moved across the page and then down to the next line and to the next. She felt his eyes, no longer like the feather, but much heavier now, as she feigned the last lines.

"That says that? That doesn't say that." Samuel looked towards the book and then back into Connie's face which had drawn closer to him.

He leaned forward just the half hair of a whisker, and they kissed. Heads tilted, lips enveloping each other, and then hands, softly holding cheeks.........they kissed.

Two white birches with soft curling bark grew a few feet from each other and served as the exiting gateway from Canterbury Creek. Connie and Samuel, hand in hand, passed between the two and looked towards their mounts that had found the damp streambed so inviting that they had lain down. And had the horses with moist bellies and knees watched and heard with human senses, they would have spoke of how the riders seemed somehow different from earlier when they were left behind and the pair passed through the hedgerow toward the creek.

The master and mistress held hands now, not as the star-crossed lovers, but as two teasing children, as a husband and wife on honeymoon, as parents of two, as an elderly couple on a stroll. They seemed to pull at each other, bouncing, stretching away and then towards one another, linked at hands, remaining connected like a rubber band. They spoke of one of the stuffy guests and Samuel protruded his chest like a cock would waltzing around a barnyard as he mimicked the "very fine" gentleman, and Connie laughed, agreeing, and then displayed this man's wife as she snuck picks of her nose, which delighted Samuel to no end as he too had once witnessed this woman's most unseemly crime.

The horses, on instinct, stood as the two drew closer. Samuel untied their reins and patted the back thigh of his animal. "Yuh ready to go, girl." He then gave a small pat, followed by another and then another, in the behind of the appaloosa as he positioned her for Connie to mount. The horse stepped to her side until she was almost nose to nose with her fellow beast.

Connie neared the animal, and Samuel handed the reins over and then cupped his hands and bent at the knees. She placed her boot, its bottom somewhat muddied, into his crossed fingers, and mounted.

"Wait a second," Samuel said as he wiped his hands on his pant legs. "I never asked you how you got outa goin' to that concert tonight...How did you?"

Connie held her reins and looped their ends around her fingers. "Ahh, yes, it was not much of a feat Samuel—I mean the excuse I made." Her eyebrows lifted, as her lips pressed together tightly trying to contain an emerging laughter.

"What?" Connie's actions, contagious, appeared on Samuel's face, though he did not contain his short sound.

"I simply told Mother that it was my time of the month."

They laughed and Samuel climbed on his horse. But he needed more. "So you let them leave and...?"

He began to ride and Connie fell in line with her animal behind him. Dusk had fallen over the trees, and the moon seemed to almost share the sky for a moment with the sun as the latter senselessly tried to hold on to its throne. They would reach The Water's Edge Inn's stables around ten, when the sky had tossed its blanket of darkness over her mountains for another night.

"That wasn't so easy, but I..." and as they rode along in the waning light, Connie began to answer Samuel's question, quite proudly and with good reason for such fervor, as she described with her detailed account how she had slipped out and would return, hopefully, unnoticed.

The orchard looks no different in the dark than in the light, Connie thought, as she crossed between its trees towards the center. She had mapped it all out earlier that evening, taking note where the apple turned into peach and peach into pear and where the berry bushes marked wilderness or civilization and where trees lined The Water's Edge Inn back lawn or where they sat deep in the acre or two of tamed fruit.

She listened to her own breathing in the thick air of the night as she moved through a row of apple trees. The orchard branches weighed light and curved upward in full bloom, less the heft of the full fruit they would soon start to sprout and the sweet scent they surrendered to the night air and to Connie's nostrils.

She had left Samuel and the horses where she had met them a few hours earlier and then crossed behind the stables and barn on the opposite side of the shrubbery entrance. She had moved past the divider where its end encountered the woods, and then, without trouble, reached her destination. The moon's light provided enough illumination for her to eye the exact tree for which she looked. As a whippoorwill sang his night song and a field mouse, disturbed by Connie's presence, skidaddled at the base of a neighbor tree, she saw the round dusked shape of the wicker laundry basket she had left there.

Connie approached it, and its dark countenance became highlighted with ebbs of woven tan and brown. Though she did not doubt that it had somehow vanished, she sighed, nonetheless, as if relieved to see an old friend.

In the basket, a few white sheets lay over a female servant's uniform. Apron and long, high-collared black dress and dainty white hat.

Connie pushed the tangled sheets aside and began to unbutton her dress.

In the time it took for the field mouse that she had interrupted to gain its composure and finish stuffing its mouth with grass seeds and return to its nest, Connie had slipped from her imported Parisian dress to the adequate, low-cost costume of a Pottash servant. She placed her dress beneath the mound of sheets, pulled her hair in a tight bun and tucked it under her new headwear, grabbed the handles of her basket, and headed for the kitchen door…

◆❖◆

The slow creak of the screen door sounded off the walls of the empty room. Silver pans with flame-toiled bottoms stacked neatly on counters were not as privileged as the crystal glassware and china plates and saucers that had been scrubbed and nestled away in the length of cabinets above them. A dull glowing light attracted seven or so Adirondack night bugs and moths as Connie placed her load on her hip and, as quickly as she could, closed the door behind her. The stowaways immediately began to click and bounce off from the thick glass light fixture and Connie glanced at them as she headed for the servants' elevator that would wheel her up to the second floor, no more than a few feet from her suite door, while her mother and father and the larger portion of the inn's guests would be applauding to the riveting finale of Handel's "Water Music."

Three-quarters through that piece as the violins roused some men to squeeze the hands of their wives or lovers, one man, who had entered the concert late with the intent of excusing himself early to make an appointment and had seated himself in the last row and aisle seat, stood up, without notice, except by a few of the players themselves, and exited the hall.

...And about the same time that Connie McRamsee crossed the shrubbery into the orchard, on the opposite side of the resort in the flush of pines that bordered the main road and the back lawn stood Timothy Wemple.

He leaned against the rough trunk of a long-needled, forty-foot high pine, and dug in his pocket. He scratched beneath his arm pit with his free hand as his other pulled from his pants the small pouch in which he carried his chewing tobacco. Wemple would much rather have been involved in the poker game that was taking place in, what could best be called, the activity room of the livery hands' house. Cigarettes and sticky cards and cheap liquor and high stakes and talk of whores. As he stuck a big wad of brown, moist tobacco between his lower gum and cheek and tucked it in with his finger, he shook his head at the thought of those boys and their antics and damned himself for standing in these woods waiting for some rich ol' bastard who couldn't keep his own whore in line.

He spat and angled his leg, propping the bottom of his boot on the tree. He had to smile though, and a crooked one at that, as his quid jutted his cheek out tightly like a mouth full of acorns would in the confined space in the face of a red squirrel. He'd get enough dough out of this fella, whose name he didn't even know, and then get himself a dandy hand of poker goin' back home, outa these backwoods, back at Firestone's and get good and drunk and then lay with a pretty whore who he would make fuck him all night long. This last thought forced Wemple to reach for his nuts and adjust.

A swishing, swooping sound and then rustle of a branch close by brought Wemple back to the woods. "Who's there?" he asked and spat. He cocked his head and attempted to look through the trees. "Who's there?" he repeated, feeling a presence. "That you, mister?"

The low whirling of an owl's whooo, whooo answered thirty seconds later, only when Wemple concluded that his silence would be safest. Whooo, whooo.

"Goddamn bird," he mumbled, spitting again and returning to his tree.

And, as the owl watched from a wide branch not far from Wemple's head, Robert Stimes approached.

Timothy Wemple stood erect again as he smelled the distinct smoke, the recognizable fume from the other day. He saw the glowing orange dot floating in front of the dark figure that stopped ten feet from where he stood.

"You got my word, stableboy."

"Name's Wemple. And, yeah, I got it."

"Anything new to report, Mr. Wemple?"

Wemple watched as the cigarette's hot tip descended an arm's length from where the voice expelled. "They was out tonight. I didn't see 'em come back, but I reckon it had to be pretty late when they did. That's about it. Flint keeps to himself—"

"Flint?"

"Yeah, Samuel Flint, that's who this pretty is hangin' about. But like I say, he keeps to himself, an' if he's prickin' her, he ain't talkin' 'bout it none." Wemple moved a step closer, ready to collect.

Whooo…whooo…

He saw the motion of the man's head turn toward the hoot owl's branch. He spat and took another step. And then he heard a movement and the click.

"You're fine where you are, Wemple."

"You crazy or somethin', Mister?" Wemple took a step back. "I'm just lookin' for what I got comin'."

"No payment tonight, young lad. In due time though, if you are in for the ride."

"I'm in for the ride, Mister, but you best make it worth it." Wemple could feel the pistol pointed at him, although he could not see it, and he felt the man smile.

"Keep an eye and an ear open and when I come calling, lay your cards with me and you will leave here with more money than your kind could make in a lifetime. Deal?"

"Deal." Wemple turned and zigzagged back through the trees, hands in pockets, anxious to wash a shot of whiskey down his dry throat.

Robert Stimes uncocked his pistol and edged it beneath his belt when Wemple had disappeared into the dark. He squatted then and took a long drag on his dying cigarette. He stared at its burning end, the rough black and gray and orange circle.

Whooo…whooo…whooo…

CHAPTER THIRTEEN

Thomas Cyrus Pottash III liked to pretend he had built his resort on untrodden territory, away from all walks of life. He suffered greatly from a conquering sort of complex, perhaps passed down to him from Thomas I and Thomas II, both men who had made such claims in their time when it came to mining or pioneering hotel management techniques.

In truth, however, if Pottash had traveled a few miles in either direction, and inwards from the road which brought him and his guests to The Water's Edge Inn, he would have found—no more than three or four, of course—but a few farms scattered in the fertile valleys around him. Had he climbed the neighboring mountains he woke up to these days, and looked hard enough, he would have knocked on the doors of one or two small cabins or shacks where man had set out to separate himself from the vulture-like advancement of the twentieth century that now spread its wings across America. No, Pottash had not planted his great estate as deeply in the Adirondacks as he had thought....

The slow, steady, rumbling roll of four wagon wheels along a dirt road is a distinct sound, especially when accompanied by the steady click, click, click of a pair of horses' hooves drawing it on its way. Add the easy pace of a man's worn boots as he walks along with his team, and his baritone voice transforming the mountain air in his lungs into a fine—but loud—rendition of "Danny Boy," and the rattling of the wagon contents, and you will hear the melodic serenade that several of Pottash's guests woke up to the morning after their enchanting evening in "The Marguerite Patricia Watkins-Pottash Concert Hall."

The sun had just spread light across The Water's Edge Inn as Pottash himself, in his brown leather slip-on slippers and paisley silk robe, stepped off the front steps and was walking the short length of the front lawn to the road. He wove between several servants who were already busy setting tables for the breakfast hour—almost three hours off. Some of the youths had not seen their employer stomping past them; however, they had stopped in their detail to see this pilgrim of the old century, one who was surely separated from his caravan, as he came into full view of their place of work.

"Good sir, what in SAM HELL do you think you are doing!" Pottash stood at the end of his brick walk as the man and his horses' heads neared him. They seemed not to notice the red-faced, balding millionaire.

"OH DANNY BOY, OH DANNY BOY, I LOVE YOU SOOOOOOOOO!"

Thomas Cyrus Pottash III will not be made an ass of, he thought and stepped into the road and stood directly in the line of the peddler's path.

The man pulled the reins of the horse closest to him, which was just as good as pulling both his animals' reins, and halted them. He continued with his final note, raising his free arm to blueness above. He had closed his eyes as he did this, squeezing them tightly. When he could hold his voice no longer, he fisted his hand, dropped his arm as if flagging the win of a Saratoga horserace, and ceased his song. He sank his head and looked towards the dusty road beneath his feet.

"What in SAM HELL do you think you are doing!" Pottash, muddled from the morning hour at which he had never risen before in his soft fifty-eight years, repeated, just as loudly as he had yelled them the first time, the only words his head held.

The man which he stood before stunk, plain and simple. He had not and did not bathe. His long suit jacket would be crawling with lice if one examined it closely. His gray beard, stained with tobacco juice in places, spread from his face like an octopus's legs, knotted in different directions and dangling across his chest and even his shoulders. It seemed to be one with the matted mess that sat atop his head. But if Pottash had looked a little further he would have seen the man's three-day empty belly and had he listened—

"I ask you again—*What* do you think you are doing?"

Peter eyed the resort on his left as he lifted his head and gave a low, long whistle. He looked Pottash up and down as Pottash had him. "Been a while since I was in these parts. The King of England move up here?" Like the crushing of a handful of yellow and red autumn leaves, he crackled a laugh, and then looked at the unmoving clenched jaw before him. "Ahh, I heard you the first time, friend. But you don't stop a song before it's finished, at least my papa taught me that. So I beg your pardon if I've woken you with the cock this morning. Your friends—I would guess that you've got a few up in there," he pointed his thumb towards the resort, "won't be needin' any of my fine goods, will they this morning?" He stepped back, with an extended arm, to showcase the array of items that hung on the tall boarded side of his faded red wagon....

From the second floor balcony, Robert Stimes leaned his naked elbows on the already warm brass railing of his private suite. Following his return from the woods, he avoided the guests banqueting after the performance, and he climbed to his room. He drank whiskey from his private stock and then drank some more. He wanted to taste his vomit, the yellow and sour of his phlegm—the sooner the better—and then rinse his mouth with the alcohol-induced sugary flavor of spring water, but when one's liver and system is as accustomed to drink as his was, then it is known that the body holds out as long as the hand can tip. And so Robert Stimes had finally passed out at four with his second bottle, a quarter full, still gripped in his hand.

And so he woke, shortly after and what had seemed like a wink to him, to the noisy traffic outside his window and the deep voice that sent a short dream of his great-grandfather sitting in his head, before he came to and wondered whether the wet in his bed was the draining of the bottle or of his bladder or if it had surged out of his mouth during the night after all.

He walked out onto his balcony to see what visitor passed so early by The Water's Edge and what man's music had seeped into his sleep.

He watched as this dirty peddler, apparently giving

Thomas Pottash his best, slowly moved his arm from the top to bottom of the side of his wagon. And Stimes, both equally drunk and hung-over, with squinting sore eyes, examined the goods as if he wanted to buy. He saw the ass ends of pots and pans hanging and horse bridles and two carved wooden picture frames missing their glass and sacks of some sort, two or three of them perhaps stuffed with potatoes or silverware or cloth, alongside a pair of dark brown leather boots, surely used by a man of labor in these parts and traded for something of greater worth, that were tied at the tops of their laces and draped over a peg in the middle of the mess. His eyes lingered on their rough, natural shine and their grooved-in work lines where the toe meets the foot, and he wondered, for a moment, what it was like to wear a pair of shoes that had never been polished, until the movement of the peddler reaching his hand out to shake Pottash's pocketed one persuaded his glance that way.

"Grimy ol' bastard." He tried to verbalize as the tearing tightness of his temples had just sent the signal to him that the man before him was the blame of his wakefulness. He turned back into the sticky dimness of his bedroom and could only muster in his head, and not across his tongue, the thought—I wouldn't buy a Goddamn thing from him.

Had Robert Stimes known that the very woman of whom he had become so desirous and possessive stood beneath him and thinking the exact opposite of his thought, he might have made a beeline for the roofed porch of The Water's Edge Inn, and asked of her intentions with her prospective purchase, instead of for his bathroom where he would kneel at his cool toilet and break into drenching sweats as he retched floods of stomach juice across his tongue and teeth until his throat could only shove short burps of foul air forward...

Not only sleep, but rest, had been Connie's bedfellows the previous night. She had undressed and crawled in her bed nearly two hours before her parents came in, and woke only once, quite briefly, as her mother cracked her door, and sticking head in, whispered, "How are you feeling, Cornelia?" Connie returned "Much better, thank you" with the side of her face still deep in her pillow and her eyelids tamed in slumber.

She stood on the long porch of The Water's Edge Inn with a hot blueberry muffin, straight from a breakfast kitchen baking tray already in use, in one hand and *Henry IV* in the other. When she exited the lobby doors and found two intruders to her quiet dawn that she planned on spending with only the rising sun and her strange feeling—a feeling that she could not quite label and had tried convincing herself could surely not be left over from her touching of lips with Samuel Flint but somehow knew was, she felt her shoulders slump forward, just a bit, as they would have when she was a little girl peering over a counter in anticipation and then told the ice cream parlor was fresh out of her favorite flavor.

She turned at the sight, heading perhaps for the back lawn or the orchard or somewhere, but stopped in action. Having caught the motion of the man she did not recognize as he lifted his arm towards his wagon, she took a step forward instead and leaned against one of the thick round white banisters that held the porch roof twelve feet from her and that separated railing from steps.

The singular snapping of Mr. Pottash's words "Heavens—no—we—need—nothing—from—you—but—for—you—to—be—on—your—way—Sir" lured Connie's attention to his tight lips, but she had seen these many times before as he would constantly smile around his smoking cigar. So her eyes immediately traced a route to the black mouth of the closer horse chomping its bit and then to the burrowed lips of the hairy man.

The pink, chapped flesh there intrigued her so that she forced her head a little forward as if looking through a crowd of people for a familiar face. Still, his arm hung outstretched and Connie's eyes and attention could not help but fall into that direction, where they had been heading before Pottash's verbal distraction, anyway.

Dingy, half-broken. The jumble of wares before her. Dusty. All seemed in some way used—Connie's eyes broke their game of dot-to-dot upon one wooden peg from which extended a triangle of…boot laces.

Connie set her still-steaming muffin and borrowed book on the rail, and moved a step down. Still under the protection of the porch roof, she allowed her eyes to follow the laces to their base, a pair of men's boots. She studied them as they hung with their toe ends pointing toward one another and examined each ring through where the thick rawhide laces looped. Certainly they had been worn, a farmer or a miner, a mill worker maybe. But their dark color, faded only to an extent, indicated to her that they still had life left in them. The size? She tightened her vision, giving her pupils slits from which to focus, measuring one of the boots from heal to toe………yes, they just might do.

The wagon began to roll forward as Pottash came up the walk. His set, narrow brow gave way as he came closer to the daughter of one of his most influential and important guests, a dear friend's offspring who would grow and bring her children to his by-then legendary mountain retreat. "Good morning, Miss McRamsee. I do hope that you weren't disturbed from your sleep by that—" he looked towards the subject of his disapproval as it began to disappear behind the trees that separated the back lawn from the road it traveled, "that wayward soul."

"Where is he heading, Mr. Pottash?"

Pottash pondered a moment, not the peddler's destination, but the girl's odd question.

Connie distinguished the source of his delayed answer immediately and stepped to retrieve her muffin and book. "What I mean is he won't be heading back in this direction, will he?" She pressed *Henry* to her chest. "Dreadful thing he was and all."

As if his accounting books had balanced correctly after an hour of perusing for the three dollar mistake, he smiled.

"Not to worry, Miss McRamsee, he's headed down the road, further past the station from which you came in. Says he sells to folks who live up this way." Pottash climbed the steps and patted Connie's shoulder as he walked by. "Poor lost fool doesn't realize there is no one up in this neck of the woods but us."

Connie gave her best societal smile and then watched Mr. Pottash enter the arched doors he had designed. She would eat her breakfast in hand on the front lawn, perhaps see if Henry had anything of worth to say—though she doubted he knew of women in the least—and, between bites and browsing, devise a plan…

Connie feared little of the time that had past. She knew that the wagon and its owner could not travel that fast and that they could only take but one road. As she crossed the back lawn to the stables, a few other guests made their way with and around her. With a "Good morning to you," she greeted the faces she recognized, Mrs. Robbins and her daughter, General Aertless and his wife, and she nodded politely to others, those not as familiar to her parents' circle but quite aware of it.

These people all were her witnesses, as they would tell Mr. McRamsee later that day what a beautiful early-riser he had and that, yes, she had joined them on the trail ride that morning, and they would, unknowingly, cooperate with the note she had left her parents on the roll-top desk in the suite stating she had a fresh urge to learn to ride after reading of Henry and Falstaff's adventure on horseback—Father could not complain, at least not fully anyway, if he himself was somehow, in part, at the source of her new desire.

More than thirty or so guests, women with parasols and white gloves and men with long coats and top hats and young children cloned as their same-sexed parent, had gathered this morn to take the two and a half-hour trail ride through their host Pottash's woods. Connie had not seen so many guests on this side of the shrubbery and she stopped at the back of them, falling into place…and thinking—this will work.

Several stable hands saddled the half dozen or so horses that remained without girth. Connie watched a blond-haired fellow, perhaps a few years younger than her, and with a small pony tail, slide the bulky leather seat onto a horse's back and proceed to strap it beneath the animal, slapping the newly dressed mount's belly so it inhaled and, hence, insuring the cinch could be drawn tight. She watched as he looped the end of the saddle's girth in a knot through a metal ring and brought the stirrup back in place, pulling down some on the latter as a safety measurement of his work. He turned, and Connie recognized him as the young man who pointed her in the direction of Samuel three days earlier.

"Good morning, ladies and gentlemen."

Connie had heard him speak from her twenty feet distance, but others in the group continued to pick out what horses they preferred to ride and inquired to the other workers as to whether there would be an intermission on such a long ride. Connie continued watching this tour guide. He pushed a few stray strands of hair behind his ear and looked at the milling guests. She guessed he was new to the job, or perhaps, a fill-in, and that public speaking was not his forte. She had guessed right.

Michael Truman woke to the knock of Donny Fisher about a half-hour before the earliest guest crossed to their side of The Water's Edge Inn. He stood digging sleep sand from his eye as he listened to Fisher describe how he had drunk himself into the hubs of hell during the poker game he was involved in the night before—and lost a month's wages to boot—and how the thought of plodding along with Pottash's snot-nose richies that morning had induced such a fume of gas to shoot straight from his ass that it was followed by a squirt of diarrhea. There was no way he could stop and shit on that trail ride, so might Michael cover for him and he would get him back tenfold when the time came.

Truman had not wondered why he chose to work with

only animals. "Ladies and gentlemen, if I may have your attention."

Some of the livery hands had begun lining the horses up in the direction of a trail that would follow the line of woods separating the road from them and then turn sharply in towards the back of the large pond that Samuel and Connie had visited a few days earlier. Michael looked through the moving horses and guests, and his eyes met those of a lovely dark-haired woman standing in the way back and who seemed to be the only one listening and looking at him. Where had he—their eyes met and she sent word by signal, throwing her shoulders back and cupping her hands around her lips.

Michael Truman hesitated and then followed suit. "Ladies and gentlemen, your attention please."

...still, the loud murmur continued...

Hands still around his mouth, his eyes looked back to his newest coach and comrade. She returned her hands to her mouth and then took one hand away, and, with her thumb, pointed upwards. Then she pointed to the corral in front of which he stood.

Michael looked behind him and then back to her.

She nodded.

He stepped back onto the bottom beam of the corral and, raising his voice, as best as a quiet-by-nature boy like Michael Truman can do, yelled, "Ladies and gentlemen!" Some turned their heads to him while his co-workers calmed horses. "Good morning. May I have your attention!"

The scene before him belonged to him and he began. "The usual tour guide is ill this morning and I will, instead, be leading you in your ride this morning." He almost enjoyed this centeredness and continued. "I am Michael Phillip Truman and will be here to make your ride as delightful as possible. Please proceed in finding the horse you will be riding this morning, as we will be leaving shortly. Thank you." He stepped down then. He never used that word—*delightful*—in his speech before, and he blushed at the thought of his mother in the city hearing him talk as such.

Truman walked through the guests as they began to follow his instructions and mount or find a horse in the procession. He approached this apparently lone female rider.

"That is more like it," she said, smiling, as he drew closer.

"Thank you, Miss—?"

"Cornelia—Connie—McRamsee, sir. And no thanks is necessary, it is difficult for one's voice to be heard, especially by this crew." Her eyes wandered across the lot of guests now taking on some form of a group that was about to embark on a trail ride.

Samuel Flint talked in his sleep, and, in Connie mentioning her name, Michael immediately placed her face…and he blushed hard. "Miss McRamsee, allow me to return the favor, if I may in some way. Enjoy your ride." Michael felt his mouse-like demure squirming up his chest again as he looked at the dark eyelashes of the woman before him. He began to turn.

Connie trusted this young man. "Sir."

He stopped. "Michael. Please."

"Michael, there is a particular horse I have completely fallen for this morning. An appaloosa with a spotted behind—"

"Yes, I know the one, she is a pip though, I will say."

"Might I take her if no one has claimed her yet?"

"Consider it done. Follow me." Michael turned, but Connie did not, she could not, follow. He halted. "Miss?"

"I'd rather take the end of the line—that is if she misbehaves right at the start I can turn back without much fuss."

"Sounds like a plan, Miss McRamsee. Wait here." He headed to where he had last seen the mare, towards the center of the line…

Connie felt like an insipid circus girl as she sat sidesaddle on the mass of stiff leather. The group had begun to move forward and it moved as slow as the camel caravan across a desert that was once described to her in a book. Still, she paced her appaloosa as it stepped forwards and sideways in an effort to move at the gait the familiar rider had allowed it to run the night before, and was able to begin to distance herself from the riders before her.

She moved along for several minutes in the tall, tromped grass of the trail's beginning, until she believed, and feared some, that the woods between her and the road had widened greatly. Her heart, then, at the thought, sped—she glanced forward at the decreasing forms before her and in one quick motion, pulled up the looseness of her dress, straddled the animal's back, jabbed its ribs, and veered its head toward a makeshift opening into the woods.

The appaloosa enjoyed this change in plan and, though her mistress had tightened her hands on the reins, it knew it had some say in the matter as compared to when they had first set out. Connie could not believe the way the horse trotted between the trees and seemed to know their destination. Flashes of bright sun swept across her face from between the limbs of pines, and she watched, feeling their interludes of heat, as they striped her lap and her hands and her horse.

The mare had begun to breathe with a quick and steady energy, and from its flared nostrils poured a sweat and healthy snot. Connie almost regretted having to pull back the reins as she saw the shadows of trees break and the dull service of the road a short ways off. The horse obeyed, however, and Connie walked it to the edge of the woods.

She coaxed her mount down the small embankment that led into the stony, dirt path. No cars had come or had left The Water's Edge since her arrival, still she would cross to the other side and ride the woods, several feet in and following her landmark toward the bearded man whom she had hoped moved as slow as she had estimated.

◆❖◆

The small fire crackled with a voice of its own as he sprinkled a handful of dry grass over its smoking base. Years of experience had taught him to teepee chips of bark and twigs over a wad of flaky dry quack or swamp grass and shove a struck wooden match into the design until it started to smoke and talk. Only then did he add his insurance over its top.

As wobbling flames reached up through this miniature structure destined for ashes, they touched off the extra thin strands of brown and began a flame sandwich of sorts. Over the pops and snaps, he heard the soft step of horse on the woods' mattress.

The animal's approach was only a confirmation of what he had sensed well before this. About the moment he turned his wagon into this small clearing that had apparently been left over from the builders of the road and served little purpose now but to wait the takeover of skunkweed and maple saplings that had begun to root there, his years of mountain wandering feet shot the signal to his brain that they shared the ground with another close by.

"Don't just sit there. Might as well keep an ol' man company," he said, without turning.

Connie had halted her horse just on the woods' side of the old man's circle. "I'm sorry to bother you, sir," she said from her saddle, "but—"

"No bother, Missy. I know you been comin'. Let me see the likes of you, though. My ass is stayin' where she sits until I get up to leave this fancy picnickin' spot for good and I ain't got eyes in the back of my head."

Connie dismounted and tied the reins of her appaloosa to a thinly looking, young willow. She had seen the man from a short distance earlier that morning, but as she looked at him now, from his back, she noticed his...his solidness, the way his heavy shoulders, though slouched from the years, filled his jacket.

He held a handcrafted roasting stick in his hand and was cramming something on the end of it when she came into his view.

The old man stopped his task and looked into the face of Connie. She looked down to her skirt, escaping his dark brown eyes.

He seemed to search…

She joined her hands in front of her.

…he searched her forehead where her ebony hair, tied in a yellow bow and in a loose bun, pulled back from it…

She looked up then, waiting.

…still, he searched her curved brows and pale cheek, the tip of her nose and the length of her lips…

"Kind sir, I am interested in, perhaps, trading—"

He stood, setting his stick down beside him, hoisting himself up with his hands, feebly, knees arguing then retreating. He extended his hand to Connie. "I am sorry, Miss. Truly. It is just that, and do humor this old man in front of you with listenin', I must tell you that you are the mirror of my wife when she was of this world." He ran his hand across his matted hair, as if trying to look presentable for the thought. "God, rest her soul, of course," he added, crossing himself. "Please, excuse my manners and join me."

Connie reached across the small, smoky fire and shook the peddler's hand. He headed for the backend of his wagon and returned a moment later with a small stool, placing it for Connie on the opposite side of the fire to which he sat back down.

Connie sat and only then saw the piece of meat that had been stuck on the end of the stick.

"Isn't much, I know," he said, picking back up the skinned field mouse that had met an untimely demise having crossed the boot path of the man who now held it. He wriggled its limp little body tighter around his stick and placed it over the flames, turning it as if it were on a rotisserie. "But I got no gun for bigger game and—"

A clanking came from, Connie thought, within the big wagon. She turned towards it and, wondered if, between the rotting red wooden boards of its front, small eyes watched her.

"Celestia," the man interrupted his own thought and yelled over his shoulder towards where Connie's attention had been drawn, "Celestia, darlin', it's all right. This fine lady won't bite if you come out and say hello." He looked back across the small circle of flames. "My daughter is a timid one, she's been sick with the coughin' since she was a wee girl, so I took to these mountains, hopin' it might help. I think she's takin' a likin' to you though, you lookin' like her mother and all."

As the man finished, a thin girl, no more than eight or nine, came slowly around the wagon and stood by one of the horse's legs and peered her face around it to see the woman in the bright yellow dress.

Connie had been taught all her life to control her actions, to think before she crossed her legs or placed a folded napkin across her finished plate or even before laughing at the words of a gentleman, but when she saw the reproduction of this man's dark brown eyes, just as large and as old, gazing at her from the long pale face of this little girl, she stood. She stood and crossed over to her and knelt down. "Good morning, Celestia. What a beautiful name. Won't you come and join us."

She extended her hand, and the girl studied her long delicate fingers a moment and moved to place a hand in them. The two returned to the fire, and Celestia's father winked at his only, truly prized possession, and smiled.

"You have a lovely daughter, sir."

"Please, Peter, if you will, and yes, she is the morning glory of this beggar's heart, all that her mother has left me to remember her by." He pulled his stick from the fire and eyed the darkened meat. His fingers hopped on its surface a couple of times before they deemed it still too hot to pull off.

Connie had returned to her stool and Celestia stood at her father's side, still half hiding behind him and sneaking stares at the living picture of her mother. "As I was sayin', I don't have the means to shoot, say, a rabbit or pheasant, and I sure ain't had the time to sling one—" The mouse had cooled and he pulled it from the stick and handed it to his daughter who readily accepted her breakfast and began to pull the flecks of meat off and savor her tiny bites. "Bein' we been tryin' to beat this storm acomin', I stop and find something for this one to eat and then we keep movin' outa these hills."

Connie took her eyes from the child and looked at Peter. "Storm?"

"Yes, ma'am, one hell—" his eyes looked toward Celestia, "one heck of a thunder storm been rollin' in the last few days." He pointed to above and behind Connie's back. "See those?"

Connie turned on her stool and looked at the long wisps of clouds that sat just above the horizon, and then looked back to this peddler-turned-oracle.

"Those are mares' tails. Them and this air, thickest, wettest air I've felt up here in two, three years—and the prick of my horses' ears—tell me a big one's on its way. I reckon' you're with those folks back at that whale of a buildin' I passed this morn?"

"Yes, I am." She thought of Mr. Pottash and his less than hospitable behavior.

"Shut your doors up, Miss, good and tight, not tonight, but more 'an likely the late night after. Rain and thunder like you ain't never seen."

Celestia finished her meal and was feeling braver. She wandered to the other side of the fire.

"Thank you, si—, Peter, I will heed your warning."

Celestia extended her small finger and sought the softness of Connie's dress fabric. With her other hand, she reached inside the neck of her worn gray dress and began to pull at the object tied to the leather string around her neck.

"Ahh, you do remind her of her mama."

Connie looked across to her host's smiling face and then to Celestia. The child's soft chest and thin dress had housed the treasure she held in her extended hand.

"What do we have here?" Connie picked up the ring looped around the leather and that lay in the palm of Celestia's hand.

"Was her mother's, said to have come from the gypsies of Europe, during the sixteenth century when her mama's great, great, great grandmother—and maybe even one or two more before that one—traveled the countryside readin' fortunes and spirit cards for the royalty. Some worldly queen was missin' that when that band of thieves left her palace."

Connie could almost see the reflection of her face in the large, faceted green stone embedded in a thick band of polished gold. In truth, as she moved it gently back and forth, she watched its ray of lime light dance across the child's face.

Celestia laughed and grabbed it, playingly, from Connie's hand and dropped it back into its hiding place. The girl lowered her head and watched the ring slide down and bounce to a stop as the leather tightened around her neck at its charm's return.

"An emerald. The biggest one, Peter, I think I have ever seen in my life. Would it not be safer on one of your smaller fingers than tied around this little one's neck? And would it not do more good to sell it and live like a king?" Connie found Celestia's armpits and tickled, the girl wiggling and giggling in response.

"Yes, an emerald from the Old World with the first letters of the queen's name who owned it engraved inside its band, Miss. And those initials have been passed down with the ring, Celestia's mother—Candella Mary Manshire—carried them. Now, the tradition and heirloom belong to Celestia and someday she, God willing, may have the chance to decide their fate, until then we hold onto them both—tightly.

"And 'tis safer around her neck, for that matter, as her mother passed the legend that only the female finger should ever wear it, lest on the hand of a man, bad luck shall fall upon him."

Celestia darted for the wagon's behind and Connie rose, remembering her first purpose.

Peter followed her action. "Should you be leaving already, Miss?"

Connie reached inside the upper sleeve of her riding jacket and removed her gold and silver cigarette case that she had neatly tucked there, and handed it to him. "I would like to trade this for a pair of boots I saw hanging on the side of your wagon. If you will have it."

Peter turned the case over in his hand and opened it, saw the remaining two cigarettes and single wooden match inside, and closed it again. "Isn't a fair trade, Miss. I mean this is worth more than those boots, more than my whole wagon, matters-a-fact."

"Please. Take it. It is all I have to trade with, and the boots are of greater value to me."

"You are not a woman to be argued with, I can see this." He moved towards the wagon and placed the case in a small compartment near the seat where he kept things of that nature that had been traded. Pens, pocketknives, hairpins. He removed the boots from the peg and returned to where the young woman now stood.

Connie had unknotted the reins from the tree and had walked her horse towards Peter. "Thank you." She climbed on her seat, a feat she now conquered with little effort.

Peter looped the boot laces around the horn of her saddle. "May I ask your name, young lady?"

"Connie Margaret McRamsee."

His mind began to search…

Connie noticed but could not wait, as she thought of the trail ride surely on its return by now. The foot of the boots rested against her thigh, and she looked down to them. Clicking the appaloosa forward, she turned to the old peddler, "Thank you again, Peter, and good luck to you and Celestia."

"And to you…" his search just now completed. "And to you, Connie Margaret McRamsee."

Chapter Fourteen

"How did you show up back at The Water's Edge Inn with a pair of men's workboots strung across your saddle?"

The clinking of bobbing ice cubes off the rounded walls of two narrow glasses, and his question, turned Connie's head and attention from her open bedroom window and postcard view of distant green tops of summer mountains to her great-grandson in her open doorway.

"How is your writing coming," she said, answering his question with a question.

"Aaah, my other unattainable mistress? Unrequited, Gram—due to a lack of inspiration I think."

"Something, someone soon, Matthew. Don't lose faith."

He crossed the room with the ice tea and handed her the one glass with a thick wedge of lemon and a small monsoon of sugar settling on its bottom, just as she had ordered. She took it with both hands and sipped. The droplets of water forming on the outside of her drink found the aged-curves and deep, long lines of her palms and fingers. "Thank you, Matthew. You are too good to me."

He returned to the edge of the bed and swallowed a third of his tea in a swig. The room had grown warmer, hotter really, with the day's heat and he had not yet repaired the siding.

Questions, like the ice cubes he tapped at with his finger in his glass, surfaced in his brain and then submerged, making room for another and another…but he found himself only asking the one that would spur his great-grandmother to continue, though he was sure she would without it when ready.

Matthew watched her small mouth, the source of a lifetime of stories…and spoken wisdom, find her glass's edge, and a feeling, only one can summon if one has felt it, swelled inside of him as he watched the wrinkled, dignified old woman unintentionally expose her girlish pleasure in this glass of instant Nestea, a drink he had prepared for her in a matter of thirty seconds. A trickle of the liquid snuck down one of her many wandering lines from the corners of her lips.

Connie had tipped her glass and let the cool sweet brown drink roll across her tongue and down her throat. She had enjoyed the taste since her days with Annie in the bookstore, as they would drink it, even on winter days, brewing a pot and setting it outside to chill naturally. The sweeping blue rose print of the pot still wrapped around her memory.

She had passed her photo album over to Matthew and it lay on the bed beside him. The photo of the Fourth picnic, however, lay on the arm of her chair and her eyes could do nothing but draw down to its top right corner. "I hid them."

"Where?"

Connie looked the few feet in front of her towards her great-grandson who sat elbows on spread knees, leaning forward and holding his cold drink. "Samuel and I had made plans the previous night to meet two days after, in the early morning." She felt her stomach knot a little as if it felt, for a second time, the worry of it all working out. She held her ice tea on the opposite arm of where her photo sat. "When I returned that midmorning after getting the boots, I found a stray patch of blackberries growing in a clearing in the woods between the stables and road. I set them in there and hoped the peddler had been right about the rain not coming in until the following night."

Connie smelled the leather of those boots…felt the heaviness of them as they thumped lightly against her saddle and her leg on the quick ride back to the resort…as her hand steadied her nearly full glass of tea. "I blamed my arrival, early and without the group, on the peevish nature of my horse, and my parents—and Robert Stimes—who were all waiting for me to join them for lunch on the back lawn did not try to contend my story."

Matthew took another long drink and felt the July heat of his great-grandmother's bedroom underneath his T-shirt. He listened.

"However, Robert Stimes insisted that we might ride together the next morning and my parents were delighted with the idea…but I had my prior engagement to keep and I did not intend to break it. So that night at the gala in honor of Mary Francis Lawrence's birthday, I did the only thing I could do, Matthew," Connie lifted her glass as if making a toast, "every time, Robert's glass was empty, I ensured a full one was close at hand."

The two mirrored the same broad smile and drank to the very aged case of ingenuity…

CHAPTER FIFTEEN

The Adirondack mountains stretch, their bold rock and summer coat of green fur, like waves of the earth frozen in motion. Dawn's twilight, before the sun is even a sliver on the eastern horizon, yawns her sleepy wakefulness across and through, under and in between, the region's waters and trees and stone. And even the kindred hills of the West Coast, or anywhere for that matter, cannot quite boast of such a successful, sacred matrimony…

Most of the horses still lay flat in their field or as fetally as large animals such as they are can, with their legs and noses tucked in and under other body parts. Some stood in sleep, but all remained in their fading night's rest. Samuel Flint and Connie McRamsee greeted one another with quiet smiles as they rounded the back of the corral at the same time and their silhouettes grew into more detailed countenances.

No words were exchanged as Samuel slipped between two cross boards of the corral and rounded up their mounts and bridled them without disturbing the other animals. He led them through the gate Connie had opened for them. She took her horse's reins from him and for the first time, as their palms past, she felt with her fingertips his thick calluses, perhaps only noticing them in contrast with his hair which her eyes found to be almost combed but with a cowlick and a rooster tail in places. She could not contain a giggle.

Samuel moved to help her on her horse. "What's funny?"

"Nothing."

"What?" Samuel smirked some, catching Connie's light air.

"Your pillow-head," she stated, laughing a little more.

Samuel stepped closer and kissed her lips. "You must like it, you get up early enough to see me," he said and then took his two hands and began to artfully and attackingly muss Connie's dark, loose hair. She raised her hands and attempted to grab his wrists as she moved back, only to bump into the side of her appaloosa in the feud.

The animal nervously stepped back. "Stop it, Samuel, stop, you're scaring Fanny."

Samuel relented and Connie stood before him with a head of hair that looked as if rats had scurried through it and had changed their minds about building a nest there. He now had his turn at mirth as a laugh lit his face, but Connie joined him also as she tried to stroke her hair behind her ears.

She pulled her animal back and Samuel noticed what little she needed his aid in mounting. He crossed to his horse and pulled himself on. "Fanny?" he said, looking at the horse beneath Connie.

"Yes, Fanny. Because of her…" and Samuel completed her sentence with her, "because of her spotted behind."

"Clever," he added.

"Yours is Coffee."

"Noo, noo, Connie, it's not Coffee. Thunder or Steam Train, somethin', anything not sooo…"

As he searched for his word, Connie kicked into Fanny's sides and the horse took to her command. "I lead today, Samuel," she said, looking over her shoulder and heading for the woods where she had passed through the day before. "Hope Coffee can keep up."

Samuel had shot after her on his mount before Connie had finished her tease. He followed her as she led him the length end of the back of the corral, then up the further woods towards the trail for guests. Riding from behind for the first time, he watched as she bounced rhythmically with her horse's slow gallop, as she leaned slightly forward becoming one with both the horse and the ride.

"Where yuh goin'?" Samuel half-effortly yelled into the morning air, knowing that the woman who had just abruptly turned into the woods with her horse would not hear him, or, as he guessed, even consider stopping for his inquiry, anyway.

He clicked his tongue and snapped his boot heels into his horse, and the two, seconds later, crossed into the trees behind Connie. Samuel did not slow their pace as his eyes adjusted to the dimmer dawn, and he followed the outline of Connie's white dress as it wove between the trunks of high pines. He too gave his horse the reins, as it crossed through the natural obstacles and was seemingly eager to dodge and stride for its master. The forest remained restful, soundless, except for the gait of the horses' hooves on the soft floor. The steady, muted clack, clack of the natural instrument did not disrupt, however, but seemed only to accompany the silent music of the morning woods.

The clearing Connie had found on her way back to The Water's Edge Inn the previous day could, by no means, any longer be called a clearing. Granted it harbored no larger trees and did let the sun stream a bulk of rays to its floor during the day, as compared to its outskirts which received only shafts and fragments of clear light, but over the years its borders snuck forth and, little by little, forest began to reclaim its territory.

More than one-hundred years ago a runaway slave, Isaiah Barkely, had called the ground, where Connie had now halted her horse, home. He had lived out the rest of his life there in a shack and one afternoon left never to return, having shot at the wrong black bear. The planks of his domesticity long since past, and now, with time's way and, perhaps, a bird having dropped a seed or two in this spot of sun, a flourishing patch of wild blackberries called Isaiah's Adirondack claim its own now.

Connie had already climbed down from Fanny and was squatting at the edge of the twisting fountain of briers to recover what she had placed there the day before when Samuel brought his horse up beside her.

"What are yuh doin', rabbit huntin'?"

With the tips of her thumb and forefinger, Connie delicately tried to push aside a few of the long, thorny vines, but they refused to mingle in the unnatural direction she was forcing them and bit at the back of her hand. "Damn it," she said, retreating her whole hand and then sucking at the thin cut just below one of her knuckles.

Samuel dismounted and bent, resting his arms around his knees. "Whatta we got here, Connie?" He took hold of her hand that she held pressed to her lips. "You gouged yourself pretty good." He pulled a small blue handkerchief from his pocket and flapped it open, and then kneeled beside her. "Here, hold this on it, what are you in there after, anyway?"

"Well, now that I've done a shameful job at surprising you," Connie looked into Samuel's bright sea-green eyes as they spoke "I don't quite understand" to her. "There are a pair of boots in there, Samuel...for you." She tipped her head in the direction of the patch in front of them. "Maybe you can get them out, if not—" She lifted the handkerchief partly from her hand and peeked at the scratch. It had already yielded from suffocation and she suddenly felt like a little girl. "I'm sure—I'm sure some wild turkey could make good use of them."

Samuel moved his head, almost as if he were peering around a corner at Connie, in hopes of bringing her eyes back to his. The effort worked and Connie looked at him. "A wild turkey?"

They sat, kneeling, facing each other a moment, wanting to laugh, wondering if the other would mind or find it to be a peculiar reaction. "Yes, a—a wild turkey."

...they uncorked their containment...

Samuel bent forward, almost on his fours and reached as carefully as he could into the slight break in the branches where Connie had had her hand stuck when he came upon her. She watched him as he moved his arm in a little further and—judging from his expression—found his fingers on the foreign object she had concealed there.

He began to remove his arm, with his hand grasping the toe end of the right boot. He tugged the whole boot from the bushes as they clung, begrudgingly giving up what they would have gladly added to the few decaying belongings of Isaiah Barkely that remained in their possession.

The lace extended and turned into a knot and then another lace and, then, finally, another boot, and Samuel held the pair in his hands.

Connie watched as Samuel looked over one of the boots like he was at the shoe store debating to spend a month or two's wages on those in hand. He looked carefully at the other and then at Connie. "New boots."

"Well, not new, but—"

"New to me, Connie. Newest boots I'll probably ever see—thanks." Setting them between Connie and him, he sat then, pulled up his pant leg, and began to untie his left boot. Connie unknotted the two laces and handed the boots to Samuel as he sat in his stocking feet. He pushed his left foot in, and his toes slid to the end as his heel found the padded sole. They sat just a hair tight. "Perfect fit," he said as Connie's anticipating eyes relaxed. They would stretch in use, he knew. "Yup, perfect fit."

He laced the three top holes that had remained without string and then looped the extra length around his ankle once and tied it. Connie handed him the other boot and he did the same and then stood.

The snugness of his new boots felt like a fine fit, though, and his maleness somehow crept in or up from them. He looked down and wiggled his toes inside the shaped, firm leather. "Feel like a new guy in these." He winked. "Let's ride."

...Connie's and Samuel's horses loped through the woods until the road disturbed the trees' roaming. Here, the animals paused briefly, but on the encouragement of their masters, they leapt onto the dry, pebbly surface and began to gallop at a quicker pace. Both Fanny and Samuel's horse kept even time on the stretch.

"Where are we going?" Connie looked across to Samuel. They had been on the road for some time and she had recognized the wayside where she had visited with the peddler the day before.

"Not much further. You'll see."

The sun began to revoke night his natural right, and could no longer sit behind the eastern skyline. As Connie and Samuel rode, they sensed the gradual change in light and began to hear the early birds' chirp. Even the pine tree limbs seemed to sway on the better side of listlessness as the dimness gave way to a low glow.

Connie fell behind with Fanny, as Samuel picked up pace with his mare in an effort to lead them to their destination. Riding this way for only a half of a minute or less, Samuel veered right, onto a small deer path that divided a thick forest. They rode in a heavy darkness under the needle roof, but both horses seemed to follow the scent of morning's light less than a mile off, on the opposite end of their entrance.

When Samuel reached the opening, he raced his horse through, and turned her abruptly so he could watch as Connie came from the woods. He waited on his mount as it tossed its head and lifted its hooves and attempted to trot in place, all in an effort to signal its master that the gallop it had just relished in was merely a tease.

"Easy, girl, easy, soon enough."

Connie, surrounded by dense dimness and left with only the confident quick pace of Fanny to guide her, could not see, but nonetheless, sensed Samuel's departure from the close-knitted bows under which she now rode. The dry, beaten-from-use path Fanny's hooves thumped along on served as, under ordinary circumstances, a passage way for deer that crossed from where Samuel now sat to a curve in Canterbury Creek at which they watered during dusk each night.

The damp, dark, almost cool air of the forest dried and warmed quite suddenly, and the hard ground of the path, without notice, seemed to soften or hold root to grass as Fanny plunged her mistress forth into the bright.

Connie blinked, her eyes adjusting to the burst of sunlight as they shut and then opened just as quickly, anxious to send images forth to her mind and body to process at their own pleasure. She felt tall grass swishing against her skirt and legs.

Samuel sat atop his horse before her, twenty to thirty feet off, as she pulled easy at Fanny's reins. His boots, clenched in his stirrups, were barely visible to her as they too were in an undertow of swaying green grass.

Her eyes, acting instinctually rather than on command, broadened scope, and Connie registered the sea of meadow that surrounded her and that spanned far past sight's dominion. Dark and pale greens, speckled with purple and yellow wildflower, bowed and waved, greeting her.

Samuel waved also, his arm lengthed high. And having Connie's attention momentarily, he switched gestures without repose and extended both his limbs outward for her—to sight the shores that nested this Adirondack ocean in which their horses waded them.

The slow-rolling cheeks of full-bloomed, shaggy green mountain faces gently swept to the edges of the meadow and stopped, not abruptly, but leaving Connie with a feeling that the grass around her now had eroded them in some way without their objection, as the waters of Canterbury Creek had its guest rocks.

Connie closed the miniature expanse between her and Samuel, and continued to breathe into her lungs what her eyes saw. The distant blue tops of the eastern range behind Samuel were not heavy enough weight to house the morning sun, and Connie watched as the bright arc began to float with gentle force from them.

"Mother Mary," she whispered, "Mother Mary and Jesus."

"Beautiful, ain't it." Samuel said, as Connie approached. "But there's more."

"How can there be?" Connie's head looked at him, then tilted upward to swallow more of her surroundings.

Samuel nodded towards Connie's horse. "See how she's skippin', Connie. Ol' Fanny's ready to go if you are."

Connie looked at Samuel's face. The white teeth of his broad, boyish grin seemed to be the color of the sun rising behind him and he sat straight on his horse.

"Just kick one good into her, give her the reins—but HOLD ON—and she'll know what to do." He turned his horse and nearly followed his own instructions.

Connie watched vicariously as Samuel raced across the grass and hollered with an intoxicated round of WHA-HOOOs. Fanny began to dance under her in envy. A response did not refrain in the confinement of thought but expounded in immediate action, Connie's hands tightened on the flat leather straps, her feet snapped into the horse's sides and she let loose a loud "HEE-YAAAH!"

They shot forward and Fanny began to gallop, Connie moving up and down on the sweaty warm back in sync with the lifting of hooves. Her senses began to become aware of the fine details like the faint mountain breeze that was doing its best to stream back her hair. She felt the air's motion as it curved behind her ears. With that and wanting more, she prodded the animal forward with a shake of the reins and another short jab.

Fanny's politeness faded and she picked up her pace. Her long legs made lunging stretches and her hooves touched ground at quick jaunts. Connie could feel her own heart thumping and quickening with the horse's thrust, but, still—

Connie flapped the leather reins in her hands again and they sounded with the snap of a light whip against the horse's neck, she poked a round of quick jabs into the ribs next to her feet. “HYAAH! HYAAH! HYAAAH!”—

The motion beneath Connie’s body transformed with no disapproval, no hesitation with the instigations. Instinct over reason. Rather than racing, the horse flowed forth now, finding full velocity, its strides like smooth leaps...Connie rode a rolling wave and, as when she had stood under the moonlight in the library three nights past, her body fluxed with an untamed feeling. The horse needed no more coaxing as it poured forward over the tall grass, and Connie felt her fingers slowly start to unwrap from around the reins.

Her body swayed in oneness with the rocking...the reins dropped...she lifted her arms to the sky, her back arched with their declaration.

...without thought, but, in action and motion, mountain and light, sky and body, she had found her own perpetual destination...

Samuel had ridden toward the eastern end of the meadow and, having felt his lady had given him exactly what he had desired, he slowed and then rounded her face to the west as Connie made way across to him.

He could make out the white figure as it drew closer. He patted his horse’s sweaty neck and looked again. He squinted. “What are yuh doin’ Connie?” he said half aloud when he was sure his eyes had seen correctly. No sooner than his lips having formed his last word did the white outline disappear from the oncoming horse. Samuel instantly kicked into his mount and they bolted towards the midpoint of the meadow...

Having felt Connie slide off, Fanny slowed her pace and doubled back, as if seeking the lost rider. The horse stood, reins dangling, and chomping a mouthful of tall grass when Samuel pulled behind her.

“Connie!” he yelled as he leapt down from his horse. He pushed the thousands of thin stalks of grass to his sides as he brushed through, looking. “Connie!” Green leaves up to his shoulders, he stretched his sight over and above and around until he came across a hole in the tips.

Three quick steps and he stood in the matted grass where Connie had rolled and now lay…face up, eyes shut, arms extended from her sides.

"Oh Jesus, oh Jesus." Samuel felt a well of tears glaze his eyes. He dropped to his knees beside her and placed a hand on her heart.

Ba-bump, ba-bump, ba-bump—

Connie's eyelids flashed to show her dancing hazel circles.

She lifted her arms and grabbed Samuel's suspenders, catching him off guard, and pulling him on her. Her smile held her rounded cheeks.

"You—" Samuel's voice cracked as he moved to get up.

Connie's hands held tight to his suspenders and she pulled him back. "I'm sorry," she laughed, "it was a jo—"

Their lips met and let pass fear and anger and jest and slight soreness for something greater. Connie let go of Samuel's suspenders and moved her arms around his back and then across to his forearms. She guided them until his hands slid between her body and the warm grass and he found the small of her back. There he noticed what his body had failed to alert him to as it lay pressed against her…that she wore no corset today.

Still seeking kisses from one another, Connie shifted to sit, and Samuel moved with her. He watched as she reached for his pant leg and pushed it up. She exposed the looped lace of his boot and began to untie it.

She looked from her task of unwinding the extra length from around his ankle and found Samuel's eyes upon her. "Nothing's free, Mr. Flint."

They shared an age-old smile.

Samuel shifted his other leg and began to untie the lace of his left boot…

The midmorning sun cast thick rays of light and heat across The Water's Edge Inn's back lawn. Today, however, it shared the sky with a thick haze, and together the two gave Pottash's guests a new humid heat to small-talk about, as conversation became a chore in its unpleasant copulation and cordiality gave way to trying temperaments. Most had taken to their private quarters today, feeling less than social, and fanned themselves and requested refills of ice water and scotch from their servants who were available at a bell's ring.

Robert Stimes could have used a tall glass of scotch on the rocks with a dash of water as he crossed the finely trimmed back lawn. He wore his riding jacket and long black riding boots with his pants tucked in them. He even carried a short, matching black whip with a small handle that his knuckles could grip across, and did. All these formalities, he wiped the length of his tall forehead, all for nothing. He knew he had missed the ride by at least an hour and a half. He reached in his left pocket, checking the hands of his round gold watch, oh for Christ's sake, chances are they would be returning shortly.

He neared the shrubbery opening and thought of what a pleasant night he had had dancing with Cornelia McRamsee...and of that Goddamn champagne fountain…and that detestable, fat, freckled old woman servant who seemed to always have a tray of other liquid treats nearby for his consumption. "Have another, Mr. Stimes, there's more where that came from," she'd say. Like warm milk to a puppy. Any good man would be in the shape he was in, any good man would have slept until the hour he had slept. Like warm thighs to—to—to any good man. His last comparison had come as he crossed onto the stable side of The Water's Edge and his thought stumbled as another butted line and tried emerging from his gut. "What, what!?" he spoke aloud, then feeling the tightness of his wet white collar as the Morse-coded words "She's laying him" translated across his brain.

"Goddamn her if she is," he said, coughing to cover up his tongue's untamed wagging. He reached and loosened his collar some and felt drips of perspiration that had gathered there as they rolled down the nape of his neck and trickled down his already moist spine.

He saw the back of a tallish young man with a full burlap bag hoisted over his left shoulder. "Excuse me. Excuse me, young man."

Stimes watched the one-hundred pound soft sack of horse grain, from the supply shed and heading for the stables, slide easily to the ground. He approached the man, perhaps a little less than half his own age, who had turned to face him. The hand's pale blue work shirt showed with darker, wet spots, and his brown trousers, held up by a pair of tan suspenders, appeared dusty at their knees, as if their wearer had to do some maneuvering on the shed's wooden floor to gain access to his goods.

"Good mornin', sir, what can I do for you."

Amicable youth, Stimes thought. But again, his innards pressed with a warbled message. "Tell me I have not missed the daily trail ride?"

"I'm afraid you have, sir. Fact is, they'll probably be comin' down that trail," Samuel said with a cup of Flint charm and a weak shot of Pottash politeness, as he swung a thumb over his shoulder toward the woods and far end of the corral while Stimes's eyes followed his motion, "any minute now."

Stimes watched for a moment the trail's entrance and end.

Samuel looked in the same direction and then back to the well-garbed man. "Not to worry none, you got all summer to take a ride. Today it's hotter than blue blazes to begin with, anyway."

Robert Stimes, almost forgetting his real reasons, believed this livery boy in front of him. "Something naturally pleasant in this lad's nature" surfaced in the vat of his thought, but as it did, another uglier, still scrambled whisper came with it. Stimes ignored the latter. "What is your name, boy?"

"Samuel Flint, sir, pleased to meet you." Samuel brushed his hand on his pants and extended it.

Stimes took it and as he did his head's caldron began to boil. "Pleased to make your acquaintance."

"Likewise, Mr..."

"Stimes, Robert Stimes."

"Mr. Stimes. Take care." Samuel bent and hugged his load with one arm and lifted it with his other.

Robert Stimes followed his movements and his eyes became fixed on the boy's feet. Where? Where had—

With the bag steadied on his shoulder, Samuel nodded a second farewell to Mr. Stimes, only to become aware of the man's stare.

"New boots?" Biding time, eyes fixed, where had he seen these?

"Yes." Samuel looked to his feet and then back to Robert Stimes's dark, eyeing eyes. "Yes. New boots." He took a few steps back. "Again, good day, Mr. Stimes." He turned then and headed for the stables.

Robert Stimes watched as the boy and the bag departed. He too desired to part from where he stood but his black leather, heeled boots did not—would not—move.

As the sun heated his body and a round of sweat slipped down his sternum, he all at once knew where he had seen the boots that this Samuel Flint wore and what he now would do.

Stimes turned then, away from the stables and towards his side of The Water's Edge Inn. Let her frolic and fuck with the horse hand.

He smelled a cool glass of strong icy scotch under his nose. "Goddamn her and him. Goddamn them both."

……Old-timers, the fathers and the mothers of mountain folklore, the few who yet remain and the many who've left this life, those from four generations back, believed that, if one stood still enough on a hot July day, at noon, as the sun sat on a deep blue precipice, one could hear a weed grow, a cornstalk stretch, or a berry bush yawn.

And others would confirm that no one ever really leaves the Adirondacks for good. They'd say that, even when the ground takes a person's earthly form, the spirit returns—as a golden rod's luminescent flaccid finger of yellow, or as a killdeer's drooping wing when stranger passes too closely by her family's nest, or as a low breeze that tickles the dust off from a creekside footpath, or…or simply as a spirit, giving breath and existence to the air and earth, animal and plant.

Samuel Flint and Connie McRamsee had left Samuel's worn boots lying on the skirts of the clearing in the woods that morning with the solid intention of retrieving them on the ride back to The Water's Edge Inn. One cannot surmise for sure—but might speculate with near certainty—why this deed sunk deep in their wells of thought, but had they returned, anyway, they would not have found the boots in the place they had set them. In fact, they would not have found them at all. Perhaps, a blackberry bush had yawned that afternoon, or, perhaps, Isaiah Barkely, like Samuel, needed a pair of new boots……

Chapter Sixteen

The night sky, with its speckles of glittering light and growing white arc of a moon, seemed more like a crystal chandelier than the natural occurrence that it was to Pottash's guests ever since their arrival at The Water's Edge Inn. To them, it could hardly be classified as fickle as the stocks that most, or rather, all of them invested in on Wall Street. However, this night's heavens, like the day that had preceded it, proved the Adirondacks could not be as clear-cut as glass or as systematic as a brokerage transaction. They had a different source of light and life, and darkness for that matter, than that of those who visited them for the first time this summer could ever imagine…

"Samuel, are we here?" Connie whispered.

"We're here, Connie. And why are you whispering?" Samuel slid down from his horse, and Connie did the same.

"The air is different up here," she said a little louder.

They stood in a clearing now, and having worked their way up a slanting mountain trail for over an hour and a half, Connie got her first clear look at the gray black above them since they had left The Water's Edge Inn. The moon's light muffled passively behind the thick opaqueness of haze that surrounded the mountains, and sauntering streams of dark clouds eclipsed the blurred half circle as they passed it in effort of their master's coup d'etat.

"HHHU," Connie winced as Samuel lay his hand on her shoulder. She looked at him.

"Easy, Connie, just me." He looked up to where her focus had been. "Gonna rain, that's all." He ran his palm slowly across the wet back of his neck. "Feel your dress."

Heat lay close to the ground, and Connie pressed her hand on one of her sleeves. The thin summer fabric stuck with absorbed moisture to her arm. "Even up here, still so humid?"

Samuel was tying the horses' reins to a nearby tree. "Yup, even up here, well, not really *up* here. That damn trail might make it seem that way, it's more like out here. And we got a doozy comin' in. Not 'til morning I would guess, though." He took her hand. "C'mon."

Though her eyes could not see the ground on which she walked with Samuel, Connie knew they crossed a soft blanket of moss. Her feet soundlessly stepped and sank, and Connie almost regretted wearing boots. She thought of how warm the thick cushion of stubble would feel pressed against the rounds of her feet and between her toes.

"He must be around back."

Connie's eyes had not seen the outline of a small shack ten feet or so in front of them until Samuel had alluded to it. Upon distinguishing its existence in the blackness of the night, with effort, Connie could see the contours of a small glass window nestled lonely in a wall and a chimney of sorts protruding from the roof.

They walked the short length and then rounded the side of the structure that appeared to house its entrance, a low framed door that barred the cold out with wooden boards in the winter, but tonight held only a zigzag-designed blanket to allow air in and keep flying insects out. As they passed to the back, or opposite side of where their horses stood, the flames of a tamed fire created a small dome of light, just big enough to host three people on its wavy outskirts.

Connie saw the figure of an old man as Samuel brought her closer to the orange and yellows. As her eyes watched their light weave across his face, she saw that he was very old, lines deeply grooved in his face. A dark red face. With his gray hair parted tightly from the middle of his head and hanging in braids tucked behind his ears and extending down to his shoulders, he is the first Indian, Connie thought, I have ever seen in my life.

"White Buffalo, please meet Connie McRamsee," Samuel said, moving closer to the fire's edge. "Connie, this is the friend I mentioned on Canterbury the other night. White Buffalo Calf Man."

"How do you do." The moss beneath Connie's feet still

seemed inviting and she wished to seat herself beside this man and his flames. Yet, proper Albany etiquette told her to remain standing until an asking was offered.

White Buffalo nodded at Samuel and then looked to Connie. The roving lines of his face and around his eyes turned upward, and, to Connie, he immediately could have been anyone's ancient grandfather. He outstretched his arm to his guests, as if his palm placed two seats on the other side of the fire for them, and his asking was offered, then accepted.

Connie and Samuel sat, next to one another, looking across the circle of low flames to White Buffalo. A small feather and smooth white stone draped in the V of his black gentlemanish suit vest that buttoned up tightly to his protruding collarbone. Dark red skin, that had seen years and sun and the miles of a continent, covered his bare arms. And in his large hands, he held a long pipe. "You have come. And I knew you would," his voice sounded, as only his exterior might have if it too could speak.

He leaned forward and took a branch that's sole purpose existed in its glowing end, and he lit the pipe. With only a moment's passing, smoke attempted to free towards the sky from the tiny glowing flecks in the bowl, but White Buffalo, with a slow steady experienced inhale, coaxed it back up the narrow passageway of the stem of the pipe. He pulled the mouthpiece away from his closed lips and reached over the fire, handing his welcome to Connie.

The wood of the pipe warmed already as Connie accepted with both hands. She looked in the small bowl and saw the contents remained lit. Without hesitation, she drew the open end to her mouth and inhaled.

As she did, White Buffalo looked to Samuel and smiled and then tipped his head downwards slightly and let his smoke exit his body. As the white puff laced upward, White Buffalo lifted his unhurrying arm, and, with hand, re-routed the smoke over his face and head, seemingly shielding himself with it.

Connie's deep inhale rested in her chest, and she passed the pipe to Samuel. She had watched White Buffalo's ritual and, though wanting to take part in it, wondered how foolish she might look had she tried it. But, the old man's hand extended to her in yet another invite, and Connie bent forward and poured the smoke over her head and hair as she had seen him do.

Samuel followed the others and then passed the pipe back across the half sphere of short flames. For several minutes the three sat, silently, and pulled smoke from White Buffalo's pipe by their heatless fire that resisted, with its mild glow of light, the advancement of the night's thick darkness.

"You have questions." White Buffalo tapped the remains of the smoked bowl into the fire and laid the pipe beside his crossed legs. His movements, as well as his words, shared a slow, graceful quality. Some sort of purposefulness, Connie felt. And his question, or rather his affirmation, she knew, had been released and now floated above the fire for her benefit.

Samuel rose and stepped out of the circle, turning for the forest fifty feet off. He would gather small branches and twigs and perhaps some pine needles for the fire's feeding.

Connie did not understand, or think about, why she began to unlace her boots. "Yes. I wonder from what tribe you come." Her finger loosened the string of her tall black boot.

"I am Dakota. Or Sioux as we have been called. The Sisseton Sioux are my people."

"Sioux?" She pulled off her boot and lowered her stocking. Her bare foot touched the warm moss. "From the West. Why is it that you are now here—in the Adirondacks?"

White Buffalo, with arms now folded across his chest, smiled. "You ask the right questions, East Woman. I am White Buffalo Calf Man. Given name by my mother who was told by the spirits to call me that." He lifted one of his hands to the night sky as if those he spoke of watched from behind the passing dark clouds. "Visited one night, she was told how the buffalo, both strong and wise, could smell a storm headed their way."

Connie set her boots, both removed now, and her stockings outside of the circle and in the dark wall of night behind her. She armed her knees to her chest and pressed her bare feet into and on the moss, and it felt better than she had imagined as she received White Buffalo's story.

"These buffalo did not run from the storm…"

Connie pulled the clip from her hair and her locks, damp and kinked and flat with warm sweat, fell to her shoulders. She watched White Buffalo who sat with his eyes closed, and she heard the snorts and tasted the dust and smelled the thick brown coats of the thousands of bearded buffalo that stood behind his lids, their heads extended towards rolling clouds, fleets of approaching clouds carrying hail and rain…and streaks of fire.

"…they did not stand and wait for the storm…"

The sounds of hooves pounded the prairie.

"…the buffalo ran into the storm…" White Buffalo opened his eyes to see Connie sitting with hers now shut. "I, like them, ran towards the storm…but behind this storm of the white man lie not safety as the buffalo knew well to find…but, there I found a body of big water. I came back here to the mountains that called louder than my homeland, that called me most."

…Connie opened her eyes…

She had crossed the continent to the Atlantic with White Buffalo and smelled the salt air and let the cool waters wash her feet as they sank in the sand, and then she returned to the quietly bright fire where they sat.

Samuel appeared then, stepping into the light. He had taken off his long-sleeved button-down, and tied it around his waist. In his bare arms, he cupped sticks and branches with sprouting green needles. He bent and let the wood roll from his arms, down his knee, to the bed of moss by the fire. He began to stoke the small flames, lying his gatherings in a basket weave fashion across them.

A hunger satisfied, smoke and new light began to trickle and spout from underneath his pattern. The fire's heat began to transform the night's hot, confining air into a drier, more breathable blanket, and the circle of flames attempted to claim a larger radius from the darkness as it reached higher towards the moon.

When Samuel had finished, he remained squatting and looked to Connie. Shadow and light began to dance across her face and he watched a reflecting bead of sweat wander down her temple and find rest on the high of her cheekbone. Connie returned his look with a long rub of her hand down his warm, wet, strong bare back.

Samuel looked across the flames to White Buffalo. Connie joined his eyes as they stared into the empty place, where the light had shoved back the night but somehow consumed the old man. The wavy heat from the fire rose like a clear sheet between them and where he had sat.

...they looked into and through the rising waves...

Not hearing, but feeling another behind and close to them they turned motionless-like to see White Buffalo kneeling beside them.

... blue paint, a line of connected bottomless triangles across his cheeks and nose...

He held two bowls of yellow paint in each hand. He nodded his head and handed each to Samuel and Connie. They took the wooden half circles with the thick bright fluid and turned slightly so that the three seemed to welcome their now well-fed, whirling fire as a fourth guest.

White Buffalo pulled a bone flute from his deerskin belt and lifted it to his mouth.

...lonnnng, steady notes began to rise to the moon in melody with the tens of twining hands of the other new guest...

Samuel dipped his index and middle into his bowl. He found the cool bottom and rubbed his fingers through the paint along the curve until they surfaced with heavy, yellow tips.

...White Buffalo's fingers, with ease and purpose, like the legs of a tortoise, moved up and down the tiny holes of his hollowed-out instrument...

Connie followed Samuel's actions and the two crossed their arms to one another, Samuel to Connie's countenance as he streaked three curving peaks up either side of her face and across her nose so the tips poked above her brows, and she, to his chest, painted a broad yellow circle with thick gold rays extending from it to the rounds of his shoulders and bones of his hips.

... the fire's heat began to stiffen the designs on their skin as they set their bowls down...

From the night and the fire's warmth, Samuel felt the dew of his perspiration as it pooled in the hair under his arms, and Connie, too, invited her dress to soak the water that poured from her and trickled down in small streams between her breasts and landed across her belly.

White Buffalo returned his flute to his belt, and stood. He turned and walked out of the light and, to Samuel and Connie, again, he seemed to turn into the night.

...the two sat, for what seemed a fortnight to them, in the globe of fire, as it crackled and talked the tale of men and women before their time...and of the men and women afterwards...and of they themselves and of their own time they would spend together...a tale like the flames that looped and dipped in and out of one another, like intermingling flames with and without source or demise...

The soft, hollow beat of open palm on a tightly pulled animal skin across a drum sounded from the night's wall. Connie moved her hand across to Samuel's and then lifted his to her chest. She held it there and with her other hand she unbuttoned the top front four clasps of her dress. She slid his hand beneath the lacey material until it pressed against the sweating soft skin of her left bosom's higher slope.

...thump...thump...thump...thump...

White Buffalo stepped on the edge of their lighted realm, his back still washed in black, his face and instrument whitened with the flash of flames. And with the rhythmic beat, his voice high-pitched itself in accompaniment. Together, the two haunting noises made music.

...h-ii-i-aay-ay-yah...

Samuel and Connie rose to their feet with the relic voice and the paced-quickening bump, bump, bump. Joined hands lifted to the sad moon who could only steal glimpses of the painted man and woman and fire because of the onset of the storm. The pair raised their feet, pulling them from the moss and then returning them in time to the sounds of White Buffalo.

...spasmodic webs of heat lightning from the east sympathized with the moon and, so, lit her view...

Samuel and Connie turned in wide circles around the high flames. Their knees raised to their bent bodies, and their hands spread wide above them. Their pores persuaded the flow of their summer night's sweat, and their bodies and faces glistened in the light as they moved around the fire.

...turning and spinning, spreading their arms and then pulling them closely...

White Buffalo remained where he stood, voicing notes and long lost words and tapping the drum's head, lifting his knees, swaying and bobbing his body in place. He closed his eyes to feel the white light of the hidden moon.

...he opened them only to see two spirits soar...

As quickly as the music had begun, it stopped.

Samuel and Connie lay on their backs on the warm, green moss. White Buffalo Calf Man entered full into their dying light circle.

Whoooooo. Whoooooo. A night owl spoke.

White Buffalo turned his head to the black forest behind his shack.

Whoooooo. Whoooooo.

He looked to his sleeping guests.

"Bird of prey. You visit me for the third night. You will not take these two. Not tonight." He sat, then, next to Samuel and Connie, and crossed his legs. He set his drum behind him and removed his flute from his belt where he had tucked it earlier. "Yes, perhaps, another leaves to your world tonight. But these spirits, one now 'til time ends, stay safe. If only tonight...they stay safe."

He began to blow into his flute and over the lazy climb

of his slow notes into the hot air, he heard the flap, flap, flap, flap of the owl leaving in flight…

A sandy mound, home of a thousand red ants that had just begun to penetrate his pants.

The black heat of the night—the black, sticky-wet, suffocating heat.

His growling belly.

While he was complaining, he would add the grumbling of the center of his groin, as well. His pecker whistled from thirst, too.

Perhaps this last ache erupted only from the vision of Candella Mary Manshire that had floated through the grooves in his old brain ever since he had gotten Celestia to sleep earlier that evening.

He rolled to his other side, and his worn wool blanket beneath him crimped on the soft soil beneath him. It was then, he opened his eyes. Widely. As if with them, he would hear the sound he had just heard, only with a greater precision this time.

…he waited…

The low, dull hum grew louder and his ears had heard correctly, confirming they needed no help from his dominating other sense. He sat up. Not curiosity, but rather the thought of company on this night crossed his mind. Someone to split a jug with. A person to talk of the nearest neighbor.

…the rattling purr of the new Ford crept closer and he saw the stretch of the vehicle's front lamps jouncing down the dirt road…

As the car made an abrupt turn into the quaint campground that Peter had parked his wagon in and attempted to rest for a few hours, the brightness turned into a shouting glare.

The peddler raised a stiff arm across his pressed eyes, and the feeling of a lonely host with open door to his unexpected guest shifted.

A tightness grew from underneath his ribs as the car's engine ceased but lights still flooded over him. Still, he might try. "Evenin', stranger."

The opening of the car door replied.

"Where yuh headed, friend?" He removed his arm from in front of his face, positioning it with the other. His eyes nearly shut fully from the dominate glow, but both his hands now pressed on the spread blanket and were ready to hoist his heavy old body if need be.

He saw feet find ground.

Then a full figure.

The shadow of a man moved in front of the car. One arm much thicker than the other? Peter rose as quickly as he could in response to his quiet, foolish question.

He knew. His legs, cramped and bendless, turned and lifted to run, only to catch their feet in the blanket below.

His throat contracted and he longed to hear the twist of a cork, but first he must shove himself back to his feet. And he did, with more grace than in his first attempt to flee, and stepped away from the slow-advancing black cutout.

...flecks of bark tasted then in his mouth...

...his throat's thirst quenched, but only with the trickle of blood from his inside cheek as he bit down on it...

The blow to his face shook his head, but he continued to lift his feet.

...the thud across his neck and spine claimed the breath he had just sucked in...

...winded, he waited, arms stretched stiffly...

A hand turned his body and he faced into the vehicle's gripping eyes. Light poured forth still, and only the swipe of the wide stick and the figure's force broke its stream.

...a sting to his ear, and his knees dropped, the blows continued to his face and nose and chest until he felt the faint touch of Candella Mary Manshire take his hand...

With the dull thump of his last whack, he stood over him, his shoulders sweaty under his suit jacket and lifting and dropping to accommodate his heavy, quick breathing. His repeated suck and release of the mountain air reigned the night's auditorium as his car's lamps burned across his back…

The smash of a glass snapped his attention from the body that lay before him to the rickety wagon parked not ten feet away. He dropped the heavy oak stick next to the limp old man and walked towards the sound. A raccoon knocking a water glass off a shelf, yes. But he had to be sure.

Two more steps and he hurriedly negated his brain's suggestion on hearing the scamper of another kind of creature as it darted across the wagon's bed and made to exit into the night. The swift creaking and swinging of the rusty hinged back doors, followed by the thump of two small feet on the packed dirt cracked against the night's quiet blackboard.

With a four pace dash, he closed in. His extended hand grabbed for the girl's shoulder, but she squirmed and set again to run. And though he missed her body, his fingers hooked hold of the leather strap that hung 'round her neck. The makeshift necklace slid until it could no more and yanked the girl to a halt, its token tucked neatly in the circle of her small neck and collarbone.

His fingers tightened the small rope around her throat and then encompassed the child's flesh, finding the hanging ring with his fingertips and then pressing it deep into her tender skin.

The wheezing gasps for air grew high-pitched, with a force that seemed as if they would suck the girl's half-grown tongue down her tender maw.

…thrashing…violent flux…then lifeless weight…

He let it slip to the ground, removing the curious object from its throat with a quick pull of the leather strap. Snap. He held in his hands a heavy stone with a string dangling from it. He pulled the leather out of the loop, and as the darkness of the wagon's opened doors blocked the car's lamps, he held this prize to the night's sky for a better view. The moon would serve no help, momentarily behind a wave of clouds, but, a close, quiet lightning bolt illuminated the heavens for an instant and the green shape shimmered for him.

An emerald. An emerald ring. He slipped it on his right pinky finger, admiring its curves and size.

The plunk of a storm drop sounded off the wagon's roof and he looked to the black above.

Some mud soon. Useful, a handful across my jacket here and there, he thought. He fisted his hand and slammed himself in the mouth, and then, before blood found the crack, he thrust his knuckles into the cave of his left eye.

The next zigzag of lightning lit the sky, this time however, accompanied by the booming voice of thunder. Thick beads of cool liquid began to fall…

Chapter Seventeen

Miss Eliza Stewart woke to the sporadic tap…thump…tap-tap at her first floor window. And as sleep made its morning exit and encore appearances, she guessed, first, that someone stood outside her window, finger to glass, and wishing to wake her. However, as she rolled over on her feather mattress and opened her eyes, the clock tucked inside her brain told her that the sky remained dark this dawn and the rapping at her window originated from a different source. Fifty some odd years of summer rain in her hat told her, just by the four drops that had fallen and the sky's black dress, that the rain would bucket hard, with the whacks of thunder and the lunges of lightning along with it.

Eliza, with eyes open, lay in her bed and waited for the next bead. The morning quiet of the mountains began to lullaby her back to sleep with its serene song and she almost wished her window open. But as her lids began curtaining her vision—and her thought—her ears relayed, not the fall of another raindrop, but instead the approach of an engine. Eliza kept her eyes closed, but the runaway train of thought had already broken through the barricades of restfulness.

One of Pottash's vehicles. Leaving so early? Of no concern. No, returning. She had remembered Mr. Stimes had announced late the evening before that he must return to Albany to attend to urgent business in regards to his new property there. She listened as the car wound up the side driveway to the garages that sat on the northeast end of The Water's Edge. But returning at such an hour? Why hadn't—

Born instinct getting the best of her, she opened her eyes and pulled the white sheet from her, with no surprise in finding that the air under it had been no different from that of the room. Warm, wet. She stepped across her floor and looked close to the glass to see the car's front lamps leading up the way.

Dawn called Miss Stewart before it called the cocks, and today, she bargained with herself, it woke her maybe a half-hour earlier than usual. So be it, she decided. She quickly moved to dress...besides, why hadn't Mr. Stimes just come by day's light, what little there would be today, or waited until the storm passed to make his return?

"Why, good heavens, Mr. Stimes, whatever has happened to you?" Miss Stewart stood in the dark driveway and watched as a soiled, battered Robert Stimes walked towards her and the side entrance to the resort.

Her presence, and her question irritated him, but perhaps another witness of his condition would prove useful. Mr. Stimes raised his hand and tapped his fat lip with its dab of dried blood, and looked at the head servant as he gaited by her. "Miss Stewart, you are immediately to wake Mr. Pottash and summon him to the front office. Tell him it is imperative I speak with him."

"Right away, sir," she spoke to his back.

"And Miss Stewart," he stopped, but without turning, and directed her, "you must also wake Mr. Henry McRamsee. Inform him he should also be present for this—this conference." He headed for the low-lit doorframe…and hoped the little muskrat had seen his return and was ready for his paid performance.

"This is preposterous! Ludicrous, Robert. I just cannot…" Henry McRamsee, robed, and already smoking a cigar sat back down in the chair beside Robert Stimes. The grand oak desk they sat in front of separated them from their host, whose sleepy brain wondered only how his world-renowned resort would ever survive such—such disgrace. Thomas Pottash could not have given two shits and a damn about the dead—

Miss Stewart knocked then at the open door and with the wave of approval from her boss, she entered the office with a silver tray holding a steaming pot of coffee and cups and creamer.

She placed the tray on the desk corner and began to distribute the three cups in front of each of the men who sat tight-lipped and watching her moves, waiting. Finally, Mr. Pottash spoke. "That will be all, Eliza. Thank you."

Miss Stewart nodded and set the pot, which she was about to pour, back down on the tray and began to exit. She was sure she smelled a rat and, as she left the office and turned into the hallway to see Timothy Wemple walking down it, she confirmed her nose's sixth sense.

"Timmy Wemple." She was not friendly and thought of the last meeting she had had with the boy. "What do you need of, this morning?"

Timothy Wemple wore the one shirt he saved for funerals and weddings, and his red hair was washed and slicked back behind his ears. His recently brushed-down riding boots held his tucked slacks. "I need to see Mr. Pottash."

"What for?" Miss Stewart held her arm extended out to Wemple's chest and she brought him to a short stop on his mission to the main office.

Wemple only looked at her. His eyes seemed as orange as his hair in the hall light. "None of your concern, Ma'am." He pointed to the room where Thomas Pottash poured coffee and stroked Henry McRamsee with a soothing word and instructed Mr. Stimes to start—slowly—from the beginning. "I'll be seein' Mr. Pottash." And with that he snapped the woman's arm down with his own and walked down the hall.

Miss Stewart saw Wemple pause briefly at the door's entrance and announce "Good morning, Mr. Pottash." He brought his hands behind his back and joined them.

Eliza moved slow to turn. Hearing "I hate to disturb you and these guests but there is something I think you may be concerned about," she took a sauntering step away from the four other wakefuls, keeping her ears extended behind her.

"What is it, boy. Come in, be quick about it. As you see I'm busy."

Wemple stepped forward and the door closed behind him. Eliza turned at that moment of door clicking shut, and heel-to-toe, silently but swiftly, made her way to the barrier. She leaned into it…

"Missing horses? Whatever are you talking about?"

"You see, Henry, I told—"

"Mr. Stimes, let the boy finish."

"Yes, sir, Mr. Pottash, takin' last night—and not in the corral this morning neither—last night I saw him—"

"Who? A name?"

"Samuel Flint, sir. Saw him leave, figured he was just gonna take a night ride, so I go about mindin' my own business, but gettin' up this mornin' seein' them still gone…trouble, sir, Flint is, if you ask my opinion—"

"You say horses. Was anyone else with him?" Miss Stewart heard Mr. McRamsee speak.

"Yes, sir, it was a young woman. Miss Cornelia McRamsee."

"Oh, good Lord, how would this boy know my daughter's—"

"With all due respect, sir, I've seen this fine young lady about more than once over the last few days with Flint, and the hands have been talkin' too about this—"

"For Christ's sake."

"Henry listen. I am as—as," Miss Stewart could see Stimes's sentiment change through the thick door, "as truly rattled by this as you are but when I came across the two of them with this peddling man, they both were as startled and—and Cornelia did little…she did little as I wrestled with that—what was his name, boy?"

"Samuel Flint, sir."

"She only stood there, Henry. They both had a purpose with that poor peddler—"

"Oh, Robert, what would Connie and this—this horse hand want of a peddler, or even know of him for that matter?" Henry McRamsee was shouting now.

"I reckon' it ain't in my place an' all…"

"Sit, Henry. Sit down. What, boy, what is it?" Pottash played referee.

"You sayin' somethin' about a peddler and all, well, Flint just yesterday showed up workin' with a paira new boots, braggin' how he got 'em so cheap from a wayward peddler."

"The peddler did have a pair of boots, Henry. I saw them when I spoke with him along the road the other morning."

Miss Stewart leaned her ear closer to the door, almost touching it.

…silence…

"So he bought a pair of *boots*, why would, why would they want to—to—"

Wemple cleared his throat. "I'm sorry sir, all of you sirs, and I ain't sure what's goin' on here, but—but…"

"What? Do you know more?" Stimes asked the question.

"Flint and this girl, there was talk—they were lookin' to run off, get the dough any way they could and run off."

"A man and his daughter are dead, Henry. Look at me—"

Miss Eliza Stewart, hearing enough, pulled her ear from the door. She turned down the hall...and headed for the opposite side of the shrubbery.

◆❖◆

Inside the office, Henry McRamsee stood. "My daughter is upstairs in her bed, gentlemen. I will retrieve her and we will get to the very bottom of this." His dying cigar, having been pulled from mouth and plunked into full coffee cup, then spoke to the quiet room with a ssszzz...

"An excellent idea, Henry. An excellent idea." Stimes stood to walk his beloved friend to the door, and as he did, he thanked Jesus Christ for keeping the bankable precocious—no, whorish and tomcat horny—nature of two loathsome lovers out so late. He even wanted to thank Wemple, in a slight way, for giving him word of the pair's rendezvous departure with such promptness. And his performance!!—well, the boy was not through yet. Stimes patted Henry on his back as he opened the door for him. "I am truly sorry for this—"

"Yes, well, she will be up there," Henry said, stopping at the open door.

"I wish my eyes were wrong, old friend."

Mr. McRamsee left for his second floor suite.

Pecks of raindrops on his window and the short, quick raps at his door seemed like echoes of one another to Michael Truman as he dug into the corner of one of his sleepy eyes with a bent knuckle. He climbed down from his top bunk and paused at the window to see darkness and a flashing display of lightning. The brief life of golden light instantly reminded him of a few days ago when he and Samuel sat and watched a different, but similar, show from the roof. For a moment he forgot of the other echo as he waited to see, perhaps, another sharp twist drop to the ground.

Huge rounds of rain seemed to burst on the glass, and

the tap turned to an urgent pound at the door.

"Hold on!" He moved from his window and opened the door. When he saw Miss Stewart, who, without word, passed through the small entrance he had made and then turned and took the knob from him and briskly shut the door behind her, his heart beat the word "Trouble."

The lower bunk remained well-made with uncrumpled sheets, and Michael noticed Miss Stewart eye it a moment before she crossed the dim room and found a seat there. "Good mornin', Michael. I'm sorry to bother yuh so early this mornin', but—"

Michael, shirtless and with only a pair of long johns on, stood close to the door, still processing what little information he had. Trouble, yes, he knew. But with that and the certain measure of wakefulness now, the internal finger began to point—"Christ, oh Lord, something I've done?" he thought and then cursed again for taking the Lord's name in vain. He took his hands and rubbed the top of his head, pushing his blond locks back and in some sort of order.

"How well do you know Samuel Flint, Truman?"

A sigh of relief. He moved to grab a shirt, and a gulp of worry in another sense shot headlong to his chest. Michael liked his one friend. Though he did not speak with him or see him all that much, he liked Samuel and he thought of the night of the Fourth of July and how Samuel's words caught in his gut. Samuel was in trouble.

He sifted through shirts and found a button-down flannel. "I know him well enough, Miss Stewart." He tucked his arms into the sleeves. "I know he is a good man."

With those words, Miss Stewart's edge dulled. Her stiff shoulders visibly loosened some. "You are right, Michael. Here is one more thing I must ask. Do you know anything else of or about him—of importance?"

Her question was like a baited hook that she bounced in front of him. She hoped.

Michael knew.

But the same trust that Miss Stewart sought in this young fellow, he wondered if he could find in her.

The dull, dark glow of the dorm room vibrated with bright as a bolt of lightning flashed outside the window.

"Yes. I know he left last night and hasn't returned."

"And with whom?"

"I can guess."

The interval between lightning grew less, and another bolt, this time with the low rumble of thunder, poured another breath of light on the meeting.

Miss Stewart stood. "He—they are in trouble, Michael. I need you to get word to them."

Michael began to button his shirt. "Yes, Ma'am. They most likely will be comin' in toward the back of the corral sometime soon, I'd guess."

Rain began to smack at the window's glass.

Miss Stewart moved towards the door. "Tell them a few of the big wigs, Stimes, especially Stimes, Pottash—" she stopped her words and looked for Michael's face, "maybe even the girl's father, are convinced that they—they have murdered a peddler and his daughter—"

"What?" Michael halted from his dressing and lifted his head.

"We don't have a lot of time, Michael, and I don't know what they'll do, but I don't think Samuel is safe if he comes back, maybe not even Connie if it comes down to whose words people will believe. That Stimes isn't to be trusted, a dangerous man I think." She turned to open the door. "So tell them to head east, towards the rain, these boys won't be able to track the horses if there are no tracks. It will bide some time, tell them I'll do what I can and to sit tight."

Michael was already turning to the heap of clothes for yesterday's pants. "Yes, Miss Stewart. I'll see to it." He looked up to see her leaving. "Miss Stewart—"

She stopped in the open of the door and watched Michael's face for a moment as he looked for the words.

"Just get word to them, Michael, it'll all work out, just get word to them."

A crack of lightning seemed to toss a tub of rain across Michael's window.

He nodded, the door shut, and his still sweaty work pants found a man's form as he made their way over his bare feet...

The centerpiece of fresh carnations had yet to be set, but the square table was already dressed with a pressed white linen spread over it and with spotless silverware wrapped in neat napkins placed on it. Even the earliest risers amongst Pottash's guests, upon their entrance into the breakfast room, would not see this setting, or the orderly arrangements of the other fifty or so tables, for at least another three or even four hours.

Thomas Pottash sat at the table and looked out the huge glass windows into the dark dawn. Rain beat to enter and thunder and lightning only seemed to be in their birthing stages as they headed for The Water's Edge Inn. Timothy Wemple chose not to sit, but stood next to the wealthiest man he would ever know and looked across the back lawn. "We're in for one today, I do believe. I hope you threw some lightnin' rods on this ol' gal, sir."

Pottash cringed at this peon's attempt at conversation and dug in his pocket for cigarettes, only to come up empty though, having dressed so hastily at Eliza Stewart's beckoning, and forgetting to stock himself properly. He was relieved to see Stimes returning from a quick jaunt to his own room. As he approached, Pottash saw he had holstered a pistol to his side and carried another in a belt in his hands. "Good Lord, Robert. Guns? Do we need guns?"

Stimes ignored the question. Laying the extra arm on the table, he pulled a chair and sat. Wemple eyed the barrel and shifted his feet.

Unlike the resort owner, Stimes, in his jacket, had supplied himself with smokes. He pulled his case out and proceeded to go about his business, not offering the other men any of his tobacco. "Where's Henry?"

"He hasn't come down yet." Pottash's eyes moved to the gun on the table.

"Necessary precaution, Thomas." Stimes blew smoke and looked at the trouncing rain.

Henry McRamsee stopped at the open doors of the breakfast room and looked at the small posse that had gathered there. He had changed from his pajamas into his riding attire and, standing there, wanted to spit on his mother's grave for poisoning his daughter's red blood. He watched the men as a jag of lightning seemed to jar them and they, perhaps feeling his presence, looked across the room at him. He drew to them.

His hand found Stimes's shoulder. "I'm sorry, Robert. For not believing you."

Stimes pulled a chair out.

McRamsee sat.

"We have a delicate matter at hand here, gentlemen." Stimes stood and moved towards the window. Convincing, I must be convincing. "You squirm at the sight of my guns, Thomas, but two people have been murdered—beaten to death—and by the time we contact any type of law up here, who knows where the culprits will be." Stimes conjured up a tear and turned to McRamsee. "Henry, I do hope your daughter, I hope Cornelia is—can somehow explain, and perhaps that is why I think we should fetch the two ourselves. Perhaps there is some explanation. If others, the sheriff—and God knows the press soon after—get involved," he looked then at Pottash, and leaned in and across the table to the head-bent McRamsee, "both you and Thomas could suffer. Your reputations beyond repair."

Pottash craved the cigarette in Stimes's hand, and his stomach flip-flopped. He looked to McRamsee. "He may be right, Henry. Robert may have a point."

Sheets of rain smashed hard against the giant glass. Wemple came closer to the table.

Henry McRamsee thought strange thoughts then, even strange to himself. The smell of his grandmother's wood stove and its glowing innards when a servant opened the door to rekindle it. His father's factories that had been passed to him, periodical visits he would have to make up that way over the continuing summer. Mrs. McRamsee still asleep in her bed. He felt a disgrace at deducing the frivolous stableboy two feet from him knew that his daughter was fucking another frivolous stableboy. He looked up. "We'll find them. I don't care about the boy, but Connie returns with us. No matter what." He squeezed his grandson's little hand beneath the table. "Connie must not be harmed."

The three men filed out towards the kitchen's exit to the back lawn and Wemple followed them, picking up the holstered gun that lay on the table and strapping it around his skinny waist.

Soaking wet a week or even a few days ago, she might have worried and wondered what she was going to do with the dress she wore. But this morning, on Fanny's back, approaching the trail's end at the rear of The Water's Edge Inn, dripping and drenched, and a horse's nose-length behind Samuel Flint, Connie McRamsee only thought of the tingle that the hard rain left as it beat against her straight back. She breathed the misty air rising from the ground and let it fill her lungs without an interruption…and she breathed again…

Lightning shot, and Samuel could guess it came from somewhere over the hill that sat behind Blue Heron Lake. The rain's cold droplets had long since stuck his shirt to his body, and from Connie's view, she could see shades of his skin where the light fabric clung. Samuel felt like the water had started to saturate his skin, however, and began to think it seeped to his bone. A shiver scooted up his spine. A cold summer rain. Strange, not like most storms he'd experienced in his nineteen or so years.

The flapping sheets of wet told him that there would be more, a lot more, and the electricity in the sky would come closer too. He looked behind him, and Connie smiled through the falling water. She let go of her reins and stretched her arms out. 'It's raining!" she yelled.

Samuel returned her glow with a single-cheeked smile. "I see that…you're a little wet."

He turned forward again and directed his horse down the last few feet of path that lay within the trees behind the corral's back gate. Maybe he and Connie had time to dry some in the tack shed before she crossed back to the main building, he thought with an ache that could not wait until the next time they would spend time alone with one another. As he turned to suggest his idea to her, his glance caught movement in the tall rain-bent and beaten grass, where tree tamed into civilization.

His horse took two more steps, and he pulled on her reins just at the clearing. "Mikey?" Samuel said, as the blond figure rose from squatting and ran, hunched over, to him. Michael Truman said nothing as his hand took Samuel's horse's reins and he attempted to turn her back into the trees.

"Mikey, what are yuh doin'?"

Connie brought Fanny up the trail and beside Samuel, so that Michael was now in between the two riders. She recognized the young man, for a second time. "Mr. Truman?"

He grabbed at her horse's reins, as well, and pulled to lure the animals back in cover. But both had wet, ridden hides, and eagerly awaited a graining and a brush-down and dry stall. They began to snort and whinny, pulling towards the stables.

"Samuel, there's trouble," Michael said, still coaxing the mares.

"Mikey, slow down. What do yuh mean?" He looked across to Connie. Her brow squeezed tightly over her eyes, and she looked down at Michael.

"Miss Stewart told me to find you, find you both. There's been a murder—"

"Murder?" Connie interrupted and looked to Samuel, as if he knew better of what Michael spoke.

Still pulling at the resisting, dancing horses, Michael continued, "A peddler and his daughter—and a man named Stimes says you two are somehow involved."

"This is insane." Connie let Michael's words root in her own. The tiny stick girl filled her head.

Samuel began to turn his horse. "What Mikey, what'd Miss Stewart say?"

"She said head east, Samuel, into the mountains—"

Loud voices came from the opposite side of the corral but muffled in the smack of lightning and boom of thunder.

"Because they can't trail us in this storm," Samuel finished Truman's relay of instructions for him and looked through the pouring rains towards the voices. He saw horses with men leading them out of the stable.

"Anything else, Mike? Did she tell you anything else?"

"She said to sit tight and she'd do what she could, but this Stimes is bad she thinks, up to no good—"

"Samuel, we'll explain—" Connie's heart began to beat against her ribs.

Michael looked up to Connie. Her wet black hair ran into her cheeks and eyes, and rain dribbled from her round lips and corners of her mouth. "Miss Connie, Miss Stewart is thinkin' you might want to hang low too, bein' when it comes down to whose word—"

A shout clearly crossed the corral and the distinct words of Timothy Wemple declared "I see them!"

"Connie maybe you should stay—" Samuel spoke over his shoulder now, his horse fully turned.

Connie, with the help of Michael Truman's hand, about-faced Fanny. "I'm not staying anywhere, anywhere you're not—"

"Connie—"

"And Miss Stewart is right, Samuel." She wiped a few strands of soaked hair from her mouth. "They wouldn't believe me. I trust her, I trust you. I don't trust them."

Samuel looked at Michael Truman. "Thanks, Truman, we'll get you back." He gave a quick nod and looked at Michael's hand on Fanny's rump.

As Samuel kicked into his horse, Michael slapped hard on Connie's mare, and the two horses took off back into the woods.

"You already have," Michael spoke to himself as he

watched the horses turn into mist and rain. He yelled, "God speed!"

Connie and Samuel heard his words as they raced along the trail they had just come. Samuel led them along the muddied path until he felt they were far enough distanced from whoever chased. Connie followed as they sharply turned, and she sensed they rode through the woods that bordered the road. Minutes later, the horses leapt from the trees' holey tent and dashed across and up the road. Samuel was taking Miss Stewart's advice and heading them for a trail that climbed into the mountains behind Blue Heron Lake…

Connie McRamsee and Samuel Flint were not the only two that heard Michael Truman's shout. When he turned, he felt the whack of a hard leather riding boot in his jaw and he dropped to his knees.

"You stupid bastard." Timothy Wemple sat atop his mount and spat on Truman's sopping blond hair. The gallop of three other horses on soft, sucking ground could be heard reining up behind him.

"Where are they?" Stimes directed his question to either of the two young men. Then he looked directly to Truman who had risen and was dabbing his cracked, bloody lip. "Where are they?"

Michael only looked at the four men seated on their horses and his eyes pinpointed, then searched, the barrels attached to Wemple's hip and Stimes's side. He said nothing, and thought then that Miss Stewart might take to ridin' with him in this rain if he asked that of her. He began to walk towards her kitchen.

"Where are you going, boy?" Pottash shouted.

Wemple snorted. "No bother, Mr. Pottash, we'll find 'em. They went headin' that way and as long as we stay on 'em I can follow their trail."

Stimes walked his horse to the side of Wemple's.

"We'll find them." He turned and looked at Pottash and Mr. McRamsee, whose faces seemed curtained behind the rain that streamed from the brims of their riding hats like water running off eaves. "We'll find them."

Stimes snapped his feet into his horse's sides and the other men followed his example. They galloped in pairs, first Wemple and Stimes, and then Pottash and Mr. McRamsee trailing closely behind. As the falling trenches of rain and rolling thunder put enough distance and limited earshot between the broken posse, without a turn of his head, Stimes spoke to Wemple. "When you shoot, shoot to kill. The dollar will be there."

Wemple kept his eye on the washy, muddy tracks. He looked harder then. "I'll kill him, I got no troubles with killin' nobody."

"Not just him, Wemple. If chance comes, kill her too."

Wemple pulled his horse short, almost bumping Stimes's leg and horse. The two other men closed the gap from behind. "Why are we stopping?" Mr. McRamsee shouted.

Lightning snapped and jutted and voiced a double crack above them in the darkness. "They turned here," Wemple pointed towards the woods, "looks like they're headin' for the high trails in backa the lake."

He looked at Stimes and nodded.

The four riders clipped their horses into the woods with a galloping run and headed for the Cracked-Lip Mountains.

Thick brown mud slopped underneath their horses' hooves, and Miss Stewart had been accurate in her presumption that the weather would worsen to the east, as low black clouds seemed to hug tree trunks and rain drops turned to liquid pellets. Samuel and Connie had ridden for nearly the whole of an hour, climbing the mountain's narrow, slippery path and distancing themselves only a few miles from their pursuers.

Smatterings of rain clouds and mist and spurts of

searchful lightning saturated the vast space between where Fanny crept along the edge of the mountain and where the next stone face sat a hundred miles off. Had it been a clear day, Connie would have looked down at and across the reflecting surface of Blue Heron Lake and the shingled roofs of The Water's Edge Inn and the flourishing green grasses of her grounds and the wilds that occupied the leftover space, but as her eyes spanned the distance over her right shoulder this dawn, they visioned the darker, though somehow equally as beautiful, twin of the Adirondacks.

Fanny's nose found Samuel's horse's tail and she halted. Connie's attention returned to the ride. The words "What's wrong" nearly slipped from her tongue, but as she turned, her question could be answered without an effort on Samuel's part. The trail they had been following seemed to end abruptly. They could not turn right, for they rode along a steep bank of trees and cliff-like rocks. Connie slowly arched her neck to accommodate her eyes' walk up the sharp slope in front of them. Hidden behind overgrown weeds and brush, it climbed upwards, reminding her of a tilted wall, and covered itself with slate and pines that crookedly shot from it here and there, until it leveled out at its summit, perhaps fifty feet up she guessed.

Thick forest lay to the left, where the pines closed tight over its fortress's floor. "Why not the woods, Samuel?" she yelled over the rain.

Samuel, too, had been scanning the sudden barricade they faced. He turned. "Too easy, Connie. They'll follow the tracks for sure in there, and we'll be so slow movin', they're bound to catch up." He turned back to the quick-climbing slant before them and then faced Connie again. "We gotta lose the horses, Connie." He slid from his mount's wet back and, with reins in hand, walked the two steps to Fanny.

Connie, too, slipped down and worked her horse's reins over its head.

Samuel took hold of them. "Listen, I'll walk them into the woods a few hundred feet. You tuck yourself low into that brush, bury yourself if you have to. I'll double-back and we'll climb that thing." He tossed his head towards the slatey grade.

Connie nodded in agreement. On instinct, both looked down the trail that they had just ridden. Samuel turned towards the woods.

Connie grabbed his wet sleeve and he turned. She cupped his face in her hands and pressed her lips to his. "Be careful, Samuel."

He nodded and returned her kiss. "Stay put 'til I come."

Connie made light, long steps, in an effort to leave the muddy ground as printless as possible, to the hedgerow, as Samuel crossed into the woods. She found a flourishing patch of wild ferns and quack and berry bushes and slipped in them and squatted, waiting…

Robert Stimes had taken lead of his party up the narrow, craggy path, and he, being driven with a much deeper and darker anticipation in finding Samuel and Connie, had put some distance between himself and the other men. When Connie saw his figure atop a gray horse that seemed to blend with its surroundings, she thought for an instant the man floated or flew forth. As she focused through the fanning leaves, her mouth grew dry and her ears sharpened to the smack of the rain against the ground and the sloshing sound of hooves as they drew nearer.

She watched as Stimes pulled his horse short almost at the same point where she and Samuel had drawn theirs to a stop. He, too, looked over the edge and then eyed the steep bank in front of him. He hung his head a moment, Connie thought as if in ponder, and then she saw his lips twist upwards. In the same instant, he drew his pistol from his side holster and—having seen the hoof prints—reined his horse into the woods…

◆❖◆

Samuel had just whacked the second horse's behind and shooed her off into the endless wood when he heard the click of a gun. He stood no more than two-hundred feet from where he had left Connie, and the rain fell only where the limbs above him allowed for it. Flashes from low lightning flickered into the quiet wet realm. He turned slowly, hand extended a little up and out, coming half circle to face Robert Stimes who, with gun stuck out, climbed from his saddle.

"You little bastard." He took a step closer to Samuel and looked to his left, then right. "Where's your little whore? I'm anxious to put a bullet in her throat, too."

"You're crazy."

"Yes. I am." Stimes chortled. "I am also the one with the gun pointed at your—hmm, your heart." He lowered his barrel an inch. "Or maybe your eyeball." He raised it back up.

"You killed them, those people."

"Um-hmm. Brilliant deduction. Your pretty new boots gave me the idea. Easy enough to convince everyone with that little detail." He tossed his hand towards Samuel's feet and pointed to them with the barrel of his pistol. "Did you buy them or did Miss McRamsee spend her daddy's money?"

Stimes now stood a few feet in front of Samuel, and Samuel could see the barrel's black hole through the thin, low mist. He then looked to his new boots and back into Stimes's dark brown eyes that miniaturized under low thick brows. "Those? A gift."

"You cocky bastard. Say your prayers." Stimes lifted his gun, aimed for Samuel's left eye, and—

The thud of a wide, dead stick knocked against the side of his head and he dropped to his knees.

Lightning lifted the dimness, and as Connie saw a green shimmer from Stimes's hand catch the quick light and then disappear as he fell, her brain tucked it away and allowed her eyes to fall upon her lover.

Samuel stared a second at Connie as she stood with a broken limb in hand and looking at him. He darted forward and grabbed her hand, pulling her to Stimes's horse. His voice swayed some and Connie saw the look in his eyes. "I'm glad as hell to see you." He pulled her head forward with his wide palm so that her forehead pressed his, and then let go. "Let's get outa here." He climbed on Stimes's saddle and pulled Connie up behind him. "Was anyone in backa him?" he asked as he hesitated on which way to lope the animal.

"No, I didn't see anyone, but I'm not sure."

Samuel turned the horse and they headed back to the trail's end. "The trees are too tight in here, the hell with it, maybe we can get up that slope—away from him, anyway."

Connie's warm, cloudy breath found Samuel's ear. "Maybe whoever is with him will believe us, Samuel. I heard him say he did it."

"We need more than word, Connie. Some sorta proof."

The horse wound through the pine trunks and worked her way back the route she had just come, and before she fully approached the trail, Samuel and Connie jumped off and darted to, and then through the brush, and began to plod their way up the slope. Their feet slipping on the wet slate and incline, they used trees as braces and moved forward.

They could not decipher which happened first—the loud boom of the gun or the flying of bits of broken shale just below their feet. They both turned and, through the rain and mist, saw another man approaching the trail's end.

Samuel's eyes squinted. "Wemple." Connie felt his hand grab hers and pull her upward. They moved even faster towards the wall's top, now only twenty feet off...

When Wemple's horse brought him to the bank that Samuel and Connie had almost defeated, he still held his gun in his hand. He began to lift his leg from his saddle and caught the movement at the woods' edge to his left.

"Did you get a hit?"

Robert Stimes stopped listening after Wemple's one-worded negative affirmation turned into excuse, and he moved towards the brush, pushing through it to the steep bank. He began to climb.

Wemple held where he stood a moment, still straddling his horse, boots pressed in stirrups and gun sitting neatly in his hand, and watched as the rich son of a bitch chased after a woman who was never his to begin with—and after her young stud, besides. "Stupid ol' bastard." Wemple wondered how the geezer thought he could satisfy a young filly like her, anyway, and snickered to see him making such progress that he was in his climb. The sound of the other men's horses came up from behind. "Suppose I'll have to walk these ducks up this," he mumbled to himself and turned, waving his arm at them…

Samuel and Connie stood at the top of the bank. Muddied, cut from sharp shale in the hands, sweating, wet from rain. They turned to see Stimes inching his way up.

"Where, Samuel?"

Samuel took Connie's hand, and they bounded across the soft grassy ground before them, scattered mists and a shoving rain serving as natural barricades.

Connie kept pace, and her lungs contracted and expanded with a wet burn and suggested she had run a considerable distance—at which instant she had—when she slammed into Samuel's halted body. "What, what is it?" And when she looked, from behind and over Samuel's shoulder, she saw.

"We gotta cross it. I knew it was here, but I wasn't sure what shape it was in."

Before the two stretched a footbridge. Slabs of wood, some rotted, some having fallen and leaving gaps, and strips of iron bracing in spots, ropes along both its sides—all, or what was left of it, seemed to float into nowhere as the heavy mist clouded its final feet and attachment to the opposite side.

The chasm it crossed extended fifty or sixty feet and fell more than double that. Connie could just make out the swirling waters of the gushing river at its base as she stretched her neck to see downward.

"Don't look down, Connie. Look across." Samuel shifted positions with her and put his hand on her back. "I'll be right behind you."

Connie delicately placed her foot on the first board and then took another step. The bridge shifted with her weight. She stepped a space and continued forward. Samuel's hand remained at her lower back as he too stepped on the bridge behind her. He saw her eyes wander downward. Her hands drew tighter on the guide-ropes. "Connie. He's comin', Connie. Don't look down." Samuel had turned to see the misted upper-body of Robert Stimes as the man pulled himself to the top of the bank and yanked out his gun.

Connie began to move more quickly across the boards. She seemed to be taking the right steps, careful steps, as the pair was about a third out over the water. But her eyes ventured down and the thick white waters hypnotized her—

The rope that her hand tightly edged along suddenly frayed with the crack of a whistling bullet. Her scream dueted with the echo.

He would have hit them if he had wanted, she knew.

She stepped a gape, and her foot slipped through the rotted board on its other side. Her body gravitated towards the rapids below—

Samuel reached tight for her arm as she yelled his name.

She pulled her boot from the black, splintered wood, and moved forward a pace.

The board her foot had left dangling opened an even bigger gap than what had existed and Samuel took a quick jump to where Connie now stood on safe footing. "Be careful," she said and turned to see him as he moved forward. His sure eyes met hers, and as his outstretched right foot found surface on the board only two feet away from the solid plank she stood on—

CRACK vibrated through her ears. She looked down to see the falsely firm board buckle under his boot.

"Samuel!" she screamed and dropped to her knees as she saw his body slip through the space—

His right foot wedged neatly and tightly, almost

snapping his ankle, between two iron rods beneath the board that had resisted his step, and his fall halted to an upside down dangle.

A simultaneous throbbing and thumping from his lower shin and beneath his left breast, Samuel hung facing the side of the chasm they had just left. He winced.

"Looks like trouble!" Stimes yelled. Samuel looked towards the taunt, to see Stimes's figure moving closer to the bridge's mouth. "Hate to see him suffer!"

Connie held tight to the boot at her knees and looked up.

Both saw Robert Stimes look his gun over and then smile to them.

Samuel arched his head to see Connie's face looking down. "Untie the boot, Connie."

"No Samuel, I won't—"

"Connie untie the boot and I have a chance."

...Stimes toyed with his gun, hefting its weight...

Tears began to stream down Connie's face. "Samuel, no, I can't let you go."

...Robert Stimes gripped his pistol in his right hand...

Samuel's voice sounded as it did the day when he came across Connie lying in the field. "Connie, I'll come back for you. I'll come back for you, now untie the boot."

Connie slowly moved her hand to the top of the boot. Her shaking fingers reached for Samuel's bowed lace...

...Robert Stimes's arm raised...

"Samuel, I love you." She looked down, to his face.

"I love you, Connie. I *will* come back for you."

...Connie pulled at the tied lace of Samuel's boot and stuck her fingers between tongue and string, and pulled...

... the trigger under Stimes's finger snapped back...

...Samuel's foot slipped from his boot...

Tightness seized her chest and head and punched a faintness through her body—Connie could do nothing but watch between the open space of the bridge as Samuel disappeared into the below. The mist and waters swallowed him, and she trembled with a dizziness and gripped harder to the guide-rope on which she now clutched.

The tinging of a bullet bounced off the chasm's walls.

Connie stared downward…warm, wet eyes searching.

Lightning flashed and she looked up, catching the faint green glow from Stimes's raised hand.

She knew, then, and stood.

Robert Stimes aimed his second shot at Connie's throat, just where he had said he would. He squinted his left eye—

The bend of his elbow jutted down in pain with the jab of Henry McRamsee's hand. "What the HELL do you think you are doing, Stimes. I told you my daughter goes untouched!"

Dabs of spit joined the rain drops accumulating on Stimes's face as his friend's words violently thrust forward, and Stimes stood a bit stupefied for a moment. Mr. McRamsee pushed his hand into Stimes's shooting shoulder, and the hunter instinctively turned schoolboy and tucked his pistol back into his holster.

"Father, it was him. Father! He is the guilty one!" Connie yelled as she held tightly to the side ropes and began to creep towards the men.

Henry McRamsee still stared into Stimes's face as if waiting for an explanation. "What's she yelling?" he turned and asked to Pottash and Wemple, both of whom had just jogged across the peninsula-like tabletop of grass. He looked at the red-haired stableboy. "Well, for Christ sake, help her back here!" With his command and the wave of his hand toward Connie, he sent Wemple trotting to the bridge.

Connie did not need the reach of Timothy Wemple's hand as she had made her way back and was stepping from the last board to solid ground when he came upon her.

Her feet found earth and her voice began. Loud, determined words accompanied an extended arm and finger. "You bastard, you rotten son of a bitch—" She approached Stimes with foot and eye and tongue, as if no one else stood before or around her.

"Now, Cornelia—" Stimes started.

"You killed them, you killed the peddler and his beautiful little girl."

"Your little boyfriend and—"

"No! No!" Only then did she turn her head to her father and Mr. Pottash. Timothy Wemple stood a few feet behind her, attempting to stay out of the crossfire. "Ask Mr. Stimes where he got his lovely ring."

Pottash and Mr. McRamsee stood. Looking at Connie, then to Stimes and then to the emerald ring on his right pinky finger. Not quite understanding.

"Ask him where the ring came from?" Connie's lips arched as she slowed each word for the befuddled men.

Finally, Pottash spoke. "Where—where did you get that ring, Robert?"

Stimes looked to his pinky finger with the heavy gold band and brilliant stone. "For God's sake this is an heirloom, my great-grandfather—"

"Bullshit, you're a liar." Connie now took her turn at shoving Robert Stimes, and he took a short step back. "That ring, nearly three-hundred years old and worth nothing less than a million, I am sure, was tied around the neck of Celestia Manshire, the girl you murdered and took it from—"

"You have lost your mind little girl." Stimes would call the bitch's bluff. "You have no proof of such—such bullshit as you so eloquently put it. You've only dug yourself a grave with knowing that little pauper's name—and her neckwear."

"What letters are engraved inside that band then, Mr. Robert Stimes, since it has been in your family for such a long time?" Connie had grabbed the rat by his balls, and—during that faint second—she thought she saw Robert Stimes, for the first time in her life, squirm ever so slightly. She did not remove her eyes from his.

Stimes took another small step back, closer to the edge of the chasm as Connie cut nearer to him. "No letters, no engraving."

"Let's see the ring, Robert." Henry McRamsee spoke. He looked to his daughter and then back to Stimes.

"Father, the initials C.M.M.—the initials of the peddler's dead wife and daughter—are engraved in that ring. You will see that for yourself if Mr. Stimes will be so kind to show it to you."

Stimes looked to Henry McRamsee and then pulled at the ring around his pinky, twisting it back and forth, at first, to draw it over his round knuckle. It slid across his trimmed and filed nail and he held it eye level, turning it until he found the cursive letters C.M.M. on the band behind the stone. He did not pause his scrutiny when his eyes read the letters, but instead, he released a quick "PHHHH" and handed it to McRamsee. He turned then and looked across the chasm... "Look for yourself, fools, there's nothing there."

Thomas Pottash and Henry McRamsee drew closer together, huddling, and Henry held the ring up, just as Stimes had done a moment ago.

The two men searched for these letters...Stimes casually moved his hands to his hips and let out a slow sigh. He reached higher then, to his pistol cradled at his lower rib. He would take Wemple first, he had the only other weapon. Then, then he would put a bullet in the other three before they would even see the others fall, maybe, perhaps one might run like a rabbit, but all the same—

He turned. Pistol drawn and level at his hips—

...Pottash and Mr. McRamsee had just made their discovery and looked to Stimes, who now stood facing them...

...Connie saw the barrel as rain bounced and rolled down it...

Her ears heard the deafening roar and her eyes, failing to explain what they saw, met the red, gaping hole that now ripped through Stimes's stomach.

His fingers uncurled from his gun, dropping it to the wet earth, and he gazed downward at the blood oozing from the bullet's deep burrow. He stumbled back, one step and then another...and Connie...the others...watched his body fall without a single sound from the chasm's edge.

Connie stood, soundlessly, without motion, attempting comprehension...

With the click of a gun being cocked, her head turned.

Timothy Wemple stepped through the rain with his still-smoking pistol raised to her father and Mr. Pottash. "I'll be takin' that ring, boys." Wemple smiled a wide smile. "That is if yours wanna live." He nodded politely to Connie as he walked past her.

Pottash raised his hands, and Henry McRamsee extended his arm out to the boy. Between his two fingers, the emerald ring dangled for Wemple's taking.

"Smart men. S'pose that's how you boys got so Goddamn rich. Unlike snakes like me who gotta take what they can get." Wemple kept his pistol out with one hand and snagged the ring from Henry McRamsee's fingers with the other.

He hefted it as if he held a pouch of gold, then slipped it on his skinny ring finger. "Goddamn!" He looked then at Connie. "Jesus H. Christ. Hope this little beaut is worth all you say it is." He sniffed the air, smelling his next whore's perfume. "Love to stick around, but I best be goin'." He began to back himself away from the three until his body was almost completely lost in the mist and rain.

Connie could still see his bright, beady eyes.

"Oh, yeah—McRamsee—I can't say for sure if your lovely girl was fuckin' Flint, but she wasn't lyin' about that crazy bastard Stimes—he musta killed them people all right, just like he was gonna shoot the shit outa you folks." The voice stopped, then with a few more feet between it and them, it echoed, "Nice knowin' yuh, you filthy rich cocksuckers." Timothy Wemple's laughter faded into the beating rain.

...as if the fog and falling wet had exchanged one for two, Miss Eliza Stewart and Michael Truman crossed the grass to where Mr. Pottash and Mr. McRamsee stood.

Connie McRamsee did not see them approaching as she had walked to the edge of the chasm and looked down into the waters. The rain dropped with less force and, through the clearing mist that now formed peepholes to the river below, she squinted hard...

...the wide, majestic stretch of a blue heron's wings drifted across and filled her vision then, and, for a moment's passing, she traced the full form, with its narrow body and slender neck, and floated over the waters with the pale blue and silvery bird until it disappeared into a dense of billowing vapor...

Familiar warm hands rested then on her shoulders.

Salt mixed with the natural taste of the mountain rains in Connie's mouth, and her shoulders began to bounce, bobbing, accepting the sobs, while Miss Stewart's touch rocked gently and steadily with each rise and fall of them. Connie gazed downward as the water swished and swirled around and over rocks and spattered probably ten feet above its source. Wanting the rising spray to reach her, wash over her, she dropped to her knees and traced the rolling, pounding splashes.

...searching...scanning...she hoped to find...somewhere in the river's water...a calm surface...

Chapter Eighteen

...cool-warm water remained from the stacks of ice that had melted in the two tall glasses, and the thumbnail-sized, white remains of one or two cubes floated gently on the reborn liquid's surface and waited for the late afternoon heat to claim their diminishing solid state...

Connie watched as the water lay still in its containment. Her tears did not feel, or taste, any differently than they had when she was seventeen. Salty and warm, and from further within her than the eyes' tear ducts. Their paths from her lower lash to her chin wound more, traveled a longer, deeper line, but, still, had not changed their essence or source.

Matthew looked at his great-grandmother and stood. Tears are strange objects for young men—even a bleeding gash can be bandaged and tended to more easily, but somehow the eyes' water is...too personal...too powerful...to the one who watches them streak, knowing no words or action can quite diminish the pain each small drop contains.

He turned and picked up the two glasses that he had placed at the foot of the bed. "I'll bring these downstairs." And with one in each hand, he stepped to leave Connie's room, thinking, hoping he was giving her some of what she needed. He halted, however, then walked to her chair and bent. His strong round lips kissed the old woman's pale, wrinkled, partly wet cheek. He found a familiar taste there. He rose, and the hard soles of his boots strode across the floor and could be heard making their way down the stairs...

When he returned, his great-grandmother had left her place in her recliner and stood by the arched glass of her open window. The sun had galloped across its sky, but still ruled hard over its dominion, and the heat rose from the distant gravel of the driveway. Connie looked across the trees of her mountains that seemed to sweat a dark green.

Matthew closed the photo album and moved it from the bed to the vanity. He took his former seat.

The same playful pair of sparrows from earlier that afternoon chattered excitedly in a nearby tree and for several minutes, their amorous voices filled the quiet room.

Connie raised one of her hands, and, with a finger, began to loop her string of pearls loosely and let it fall back to her chest. "When we returned to The Water's Edge Inn that morning, the library wing was ablaze from where lightning had struck it. Everyone was in a frenzy...Pottash nearly had a heart attack then and there." Connie talked, voice low, towards the window, and Matthew leaned in to listen. "Our absence had not been missed all that much because of it and it was all that much easier for my father and Pottash to dismiss, the best they could, all that had happened and move on to the more important matter at hand. That afternoon my father drove me back to Albany and three days later I was heading for Ireland to stay with his sisters."

Matthew watched his great-grandmother's eyes follow the route of her ship across the mountains.

"I was...was to stay there for an indefinite period of time, and I waited, perhaps for some word from Samuel, a letter...anything...I walked the coast some days searching it for his arrival. Months passed, and nothing...no one. A year later, Mother took ill and Father wrote for me to be returned. They had bought this estate and I came back. In a stack of mail, our maid had set aside for me...there was a letter dated shortly after I had left for Ireland."

Connie stopped and Matthew waited. He saw the in and out of her small frame as she turned the warm air over in her lungs and breathed. She drew her bent finger from the wrap of beads and let the necklace take form again. It remained there then.

"It was from Eliza Stewart...she had written to tell me that Michael Truman had received a visit from an old Indian man on the stable grounds."

Matthew listened with ears and eyes and body.

"White Buffalo told him that Samuel had come...more dead than alive...and collapsed at his cabin...the bullet had grazed him badly, and he had lost blood. A lot of blood." She turned then and looked at her great-grandson. "He died that night."

Tears are too personal and too powerful, and Matthew was not sure how his chest could weigh so heavy for a man who died almost a century ago. He knew, though, that there is always more to matters of the heart. He looked across to Connie's chair and saw the black and white still sitting on the arm. He got up and brought the photo to the nightstand, propping it up on the round face of Connie's alarm clock.

Connie's eyes watched and smiled as he did so, and then the old woman peered out her window again, this time tracing the still leaf of one of the maples in the yard. She felt the strong warm hand on her shoulder and did not turn, but only raised her own tired one to it and patted, then squeezed, the chapped knuckles and hard fingers she found there.

…and time, just then, though never given any justice, was hardly noted or scaled or neatly packaged in the click, click, click of the red second-hand on the nearby clock…

Matthew slipped his hand from underneath Connie's, picked up his hammer and the few nails that he had set beside the nightstand, and turned to go. "I'll leave that ladder there and finish up tomorrow, Gram."

She heard his receding steps. "Matthew."

He stopped.

"Matthew, take that cane of your grandmother Samantha's and—and place it under my bed, would you?"

Without words, Matthew looked at the cane that had been leaning on the nightstand and then followed his great-grandmother's wishes…

He rose from the floor and his task, then. "Connie?"

"Yes."

"Is Samantha…I mean her name is so close—or similar—to Samuel."

"No, Matthew. She isn't. But, in Ireland, I told myself… in the one and only short second of waning faith I ever experienced there…that if Samuel did not come back for me as he had promised I would name my firstborn for him, be it a boy or a girl. Samantha is so much…"

Matthew waited for her to finish, but she only continued to look out her window. "See you tomorrow, Connie," he said and left.

Connie watched a wad of white crest over the green and blue peaks. She saw Matthew walk down her driveway and get into his truck and drive away. She heard the conversation of her sparrows as they moved and now took a dust bath in the dry ground beneath her maples. She counted the different shades of blue in the summer sky…

…July in early bloom does not heed darkness its true deserved respect, as it pokes it with countless specks of light, trying to diminish its character.

Connie's vision bounced from star to star, and she still had not learned the names of all the constellations but at the same time considered herself no less of an Adirondackian for it. The air remained warm and an inviting breeze begged her to leave her window open. She leaned against the frame one more moment, arms lightly crossed. The pale blue of her long nightgown matched the low horizon of the night sky, and she took and tasted in one last deep breath and crossed the room to her bed…

…bump…bump…bump…

Feet climbing the rungs of the ladder outside her window brought her eyes to an open, and she lay still, hearing each step grow louder and nearer until the ascender was no longer an assumption but a presence that could be felt.

"Who's there?" she asked, sitting up, her back somehow oddly curving down to her buttocks and finding the mattress much softer. And even her voice? Her eyes adjusted to the darkness and she fingered a lock of hair behind her ear—

The hair smooth…the finger's touch softer to the ear?

"'If I profane with my unworthiest hand/This holy shrine, the gentle sin is this'—still don't know what that means," the intruder answered.

…the voice…

Connie flapped the sheet from her body.

"'My lips, two blushing pilgrims, ready stand/To smooth that rough touch with a tender kiss'—looks like you're in trouble, Connie."

Her bare feet found the warm surface of her hard oak floor and she stepped to the window with her hands outstretched to cup the face there in the dark.

Their mouths ran across each others and dabbed and grabbed for the pink softness they found.

"I told yuh—"

Their lips continued to bounce off each other's. Connie's eyes watered.

"I told yuh I would come back," he said.

"Well, it took you long enough." Connie moved back a

foot from the window to see if her senses had not left her.

Samuel Flint rose three more rungs on the ladder and entered through the window...boots first. When he climbed into her room and stood fully in front of her, his tall body and sort of wide shoulders and suspenders and new boots, she moved and sat at the head of her bed, by her nightstand, and could only laugh.

He swelled inside, too, as he stood before her and lost his hands in her wavy locks and allowed his eyes to search the bright hazel of hers cresting on her high, smooth cheekbones. He reached in his pocket then. "Somebody asked me to give this to you." He leaned forward and kissed Connie on the forehead, pulled out a shiny object, and then sat beside her on the bed.

"My cigarette case." Connie accepted it and turned it over in her hands, as if making sure of its authenticity. "My cigarette case." She snapped it open and two cigarettes and a wooden match remained, as when she had traded it.

Samuel reached in it and placed the two cigarettes in his mouth. He picked up the match and Connie snapped the case shut and looked to him. He ran the little wooden stick across the swirly silver and gold surface.

The flame, as the match's head ignited, started small and then burst into light, blue at its base and then yellow and bright orange, and its flicker danced across the walls of Connie's room.

Samuel drew it to his face and lit the cigarettes, handing one to Connie. He did not flutter the flame out, however, but, on seeing Connie reopen the cigarette case to serve as an ashtray and then set it on her nightstand, he placed it there in the bright box and, together, they watched its waves of colors reflect off the glowing innerwalls...

Afterword
July 1998

Now, four years after the death of my great-grandmother Connie McRamsee Prauffette, and nearly a century after her visit to The Water's Edge Inn and her romance with Samuel Flint, I sit, in her bedroom, my bedroom now as I have taken over her property here in the Adirondack Mountains, and write the last words to the novel inspired by and told from an old woman's heart.

Two years to write and revise and another two to find a publisher, her story finds print this summer with a small Adirondack publishing company, the same one, somewhat ironically, that, in 1955, published a small book of letters written by a then middle-aged Michael Truman.

And these days, people are kind enough to compliment me on my work and say things like "Fine piece of fiction, Matthew. It is fiction, isn't it?" I smile and say "Yes, it is fiction" and know that nothing is ever completely fiction, just as nothing is ever completely truth.

My grandmother Samantha took Connie's death as would be expected, but some time after, she started counseling young women involved in alcoholic relationships and, perhaps, or better said, I believe, has found some core truth, as my great-grandmother had always hoped she would.

MaryAnn called when she got word my book was being published. She said she has a child, a daughter, and now lives with a man. We spoke of everything but our truth, and, sometimes, it is that way.

But I cannot complain, as my other love did come calling. On my desk, next to my early model word processor, in a silver and gold cigarette case, I keep a small black and white photograph of a Fourth of July picnic taken around the turn of the century, two cigarette butts, and the fire of my inspiration.

—Matthew Alstrade

Acknowledgements

Books do not write themselves.

Writers do not write themselves, either. People nurture them, feed them, encourage them, believe in them, deflate them and blow them back up again, watch them wallow in self-pity and swim in self-absorption and fly high in selflessness, become fed up with them and then put up with them, put them down and listen to their runarounds, become the sacrificial element of their daily ritual in the face of their craft…their love…their passion. These are the people who share the vision.

My greatest thanks to the following people who have shared my vision and let me know that I am truly very blessed:

My sisters, the souls of three strong women, Caitlyn who follows their footsteps; Karen, support does not describe; my parents, you have given me the faith; Mere, you do it for me; Charlotte Zoe Walker, my mentor, you shifted my path; Patrick Meanor, an amazing human being with endless interest and care; Pam Collins, for "The Ax," words I live by; the O-State crew, "To distance…"; Marti, the first to read, the finder of Antonio Santana—the man who turned word into art; Buck and James, all those stories in the bathroom, all those rejections, there from the beginning of a dream; the boys from home, especially Flick, tech wizard, and the late Dominic who taught all of us to laugh a little bit harder; JC Himself, paving the way…

The list could go on, but the orchestra has started to play. To everyone that cared enough to ask—

new boots is a reality. Thank you, again.

Louis J. Fagan

Book Ordering Information

Additional copies of new boots by louis j. fagan can be obtained by using the order form below.

Qty	Publication	Unit Cost	Total
	new boots	$11.95	

New York residents add 7% sales tax		$
Shipping and handling	$3.00 per book	$
Total		$

Please mail check or money order (sorry, no CODs) and make payable to:

A-Peak Publishing
P.O. Box 511
Johnstown, NY 12095

Name ______________________________

Address ______________________________

City ____________________ State ________ Zip ______

Please allow 4-6 weeks for delivery. Prices subject to change without notice. Payment in U.S. funds only. New York residents add applicable sales tax.

Need additional order forms?
Have questions or comments?
Please contact us at
apeak@superior.net

Thank you.